MAHITA VAS

It Happened on Scrabble Sunday

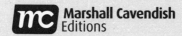

Marshall Cavendish
Editions

Published by Marshall Cavendish Editions
An imprint of Marshall Cavendish International

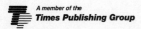

A member of the
Times Publishing Group

Other Marshall Cavendish Offices:
Marshall Cavendish Corporation. 99 White Plains Road, Tarrytown NY 10591-9001, USA • Marshall Cavendish International (Thailand) Co Ltd. 253 Asoke, 12th Floor, Sukhumvit 21 Road, Klongtoey Nua, Wattana, Bangkok 10110, Thailand • Marshall Cavendish (Malaysia) Sdn Bhd, Times Subang, Lot 46, Subang Hi-Tech Industrial Park, Batu Tiga, 40000 Shah Alam, Selangor Darul Ehsan, Malaysia

Marshall Cavendish is a registered trademark of Times Publishing Limited.

National Library Board, Singapore Cataloguing-in-Publication Data

Name(s): Vas, Mahita.
Title: It happened on Scrabble Sunday / Mahita Vas.
Description: Singapore : Marshall Cavendish Editions, [2018]
Identifier(s): OCN 1036844133 | ISBN 978-981-47-9476-3 (paperback)
Subject(s): LCSH: Murder--Fiction. | Revenge--Fiction.
Classification: DDC S823--dc23

Printed in Singapore

For my family –
Michael, Lindsay and Claire

Four hours. That's how long I've been sitting in this room, the intensive care unit at Temasek University Hospital. For four excruciating hours I have been watching my child as she lies hooked up to monitors and a respirator, suspended between life and death.

The nurses whisper, as if in the dead of night spirits might hear them and jinx their patient's chances of recovery. It is generally believed that the hospital is haunted, having been built on the grounds of a massacre site during the Japanese occupation. I haven't been in this room long enough to notice ghosts eavesdropping.

"So young, so beautiful," says the older nurse, a matronly Chinese woman. She shakes her head and sighs as she checks the drip. "Such a waste."

"Maybe she'll make it. We've seen that happen. I'm praying for her," says the younger nurse, a scrawny, dark-skinned woman from Myanmar.

"You pray for all your patients? You Christian or Buddhist?"

"Christian. Ya, I pray for all my patients. Every day, ever since I became a nurse."

"But still some die. Or never wake up. Like that, pray for what?"

The younger nurse is silent. She takes Lavinia's pulse, murmurs a few words—is it a prayer?—and leaves the room, a look of smugness plastered across her tanned face. She seems sweet-natured and clearly filled with good intentions, but I am curious; the next time she comes in, I'm going to ask her about her god, the one that allowed such evil to befall my child.

I was there. I saw it happen. First, Lavinia called for me, "Mama! Come, Mama! Help me!" but the men were too strong. I could not stop them. Lavinia began to recite the prayer she said at the start and end of every day, ever since she became a Catholic during her first year in university. She repeated the Hail Mary seven times, like a pre-recorded loop. With each repetition, her breathing became more rapid and her voice became more shrill. By the time I managed to push the skinny one away, Lavinia had passed out. Whether there is a god or not, last night I witnessed first-hand the triumph of evil over good.

My beloved Lavinia will wake up soon. She hasn't opened her eyes yet, but whenever I say her name while I hold her hand, I feel a stirring inside. And she still speaks to me. Mischievous child, deliberately confounding the doctors. *Open your eyes, say a few words while they're here,* I tell her. *Then they'll put you on that scale they use to determine your chances of recovery. It will give your father and brothers hope.*

She doesn't always respond, but I know she can hear me.

I stand next to her and stroke her face, swollen on the left, her pale skin mottled with shades of deep red and blue, interspersed with patches of black. Pus is seeping through the bandage on her right cheek. *My beautiful child. You'll wake up soon. You always loved fairy tales. You'll be the princess who wakes up.*

PART I

1

The Previous Night

Uday sat up, pushing his hands into the cushions and hitting his heels against the base of the sofa. He blinked for a few seconds before realising he had dozed off. He could not remember the last time anyone had used the land line. It was probably a wrong number. The ringtone had to be changed; Lavinia had chosen a classical piece from when she was learning to play the violin. It was a piercing sound and bore no relation to *Pachelbel's Canon,* but Lavinia, eight at the time, had been insistent. Uday recognised the number.

"Lavi, I've been so worried!" Uday heard background sounds and breathing. "Lavi? Are you okay? Hello? Hello?" Uday grabbed the remote control and switched off the television as he pressed the cordless phone against his ear.

"What did you say? Who are you? Is this some sick joke?" Trembling, Uday searched for a pen and paper. He repeated the address as he scribbled it on the thin, white paper. He glanced at his watch. Nearly eleven. "I'll be there right away."

Ashwin and Sayana sprinted to Uday's flat as soon as they received Uday's Whatsapp message. As they walked into their father's bedroom, they saw him zipping up a sports bag.

Uday threw his keys towards Sayana. "Get the car and meet

me in the driveway." As Sayana rushed out of the room, Uday reached into his pocket and handed Ashwin a crushed piece of paper. "Tell Sayana to plug this address into the GPS. Go!"

Uday opened the safe to see if there was anything left in there. He slammed the door shut, grabbed the sports bag and left without locking the empty safe.

Ashwin got out of the back seat to open the front door for his father but Uday insisted on Ashwin sitting in front with Sayana. The brothers had bickered all evening. Lifting his bag, he said, "I'd like to go through these things. Just sit with your brother, please." It seemed like a reasonable excuse and Ashwin obliged. The two boys could transform into imbeciles at the slightest provocation, but he knew that in times of trouble he could trust them to look out for one another.

"What's in that bag, Dad? What's going on?" Ashwin held the seat belt away from him, to prevent it from cutting into his neck as he turned to face his father.

"They have Lavi. She's been hurt and is being held hostage—" Sayana slowed down. "Hostage? By whom? Why?"

"Keep going Sayana! We don't have much time."

"We should call the police."

"No! We won't involve the police. The fellow who called promised she'll be okay and warned against calling the police. His English was terrible, but I understood this much. Someone wanted her dead, but he saved her. Didn't claim to be a hero or anything. Just said he saved her and she'll be okay. Any sign of the cops and she may not be … she definitely won't … be okay."

Uday removed the leather jewellery case from his bag and opened it with a loud click. He removed the diamond bracelet from a deep, narrow, velvet-lined slot.

"Aren't those Mama's jewels? The diamonds you said would go to Lavinia when she gets married?"

Uday put the bracelet back into the box and moved it away from him. "Yes. There is something vulgar about using these diamonds to buy our Lavi's freedom." Uday glanced at the box in the dark.

"How much did they ask for?"

"Sounded like it was just one man. He asked for a million ringgit—"

Ashwin gasped. "He's Malaysian! I hope they haven't taken Lavi to Malaysia."

Sayana used his know-it-all voice to reassure them. "Not that easy these days. The officers on both sides of the causeway seem to be on perpetually high alert, thank goodness."

Uday continued, "I told him that this late at night no one can get hold of that kind of money—I think it's about three hundred and fifty thousand dollars these days. He then said to bring whatever I had, but he wanted nothing less than a hundred thousand dollars. Cash, watches, jewellery. He said all rich people have at least this much at home, and I shot back that this wasn't Malaysia where rich people hid their dirty money in vaults."

Ashwin thrust his chin towards the bag. "Do you have that much in there, Dad? It's ransom. He's not saving Lavi. He's selling her life!"

"I don't think she was just kidnapped for ransom. This fellow, he … he said …" Uday sucked in enough air to bloat his face before releasing a loud exhalation filled with fear and anger. "He said he was paid to kill her but will release her alive if I pay him. He needs the money to start a new life in Malaysia." Uday looked at his watch, a Rolex Daytona with a rose gold bezel and a patented black bracelet. He looked out of the window as he unclasped the bracelet and slid the watch off his hand.

"Dad, you have at least ten other watches. Why part with your favourite? And it's just months old!"

"My favourite is also my most expensive, and means nothing in exchange for my darling daughter."

Uday opened the velvet jewellery box and selected a few pieces—a heavy gold necklace, bought for Julie when they first moved to Singapore; a sapphire and diamond bracelet, a gift for Julie when Lavinia was born; and a pair of earrings, flawless diamond solitaires in D colour, at least two carats each; and placed them next to the watch.

"A lot more than a hundred thousand dollars' worth here. Assuming he gets screwed selling the watch and these earrings—and damn, why should I care—he should still get fifty grand. Plus, all this." Uday reached into the bottom of the gym bag and brought out several stacks of notes in an all-too-familiar green. "Fifty thousand US dollars. Five thick stacks of hundred-dollar bills should make the bastard happy."

"Why are you giving him so much? Wouldn't fifty grand Singapore dollars in cash and fifty in jewellery, actually worth a hundred to start with, be plenty?"

"This is my Lavi. I will give more than what's expected just to have her back with us."

Sayana looked at his Dad in the rear-view mirror. "Fine. But tell us, Dad. Why do you have so much cash lying around the house? Please don't tell us it's dirty money!"

Uday's expression changed. He put his hand to his heart and said in a soft voice, "After everything I have taught you about honesty, decency and integrity, I cannot believe you just said that to me. No, Sayana, this money is clean. Sterile. This was meant for a down payment on a house in Penang. The owner wanted cash for the first payment. Apparently, Stamford Raffles spent a week there, at the home of an acquaintance. I was going to fly to Penang with Tamara next weekend. But she had to rush back to Shanghai."

As they took the Paya Lebar exit, Ashwin asked, "What the hell are they doing at an industrial estate? This whole Ubi area is full of factories."

Uday looked out of the window on both sides. "I don't know. It sounded like whoever is helping, or appearing to help save Lavi, is in fact double-crossing the real culprit."

They found the building after a detour that had not been updated on the GPS. Finding the front entrance shuttered, Sayana drove to the empty carpark at the back and knocked on the wide wooden door to the back entrance. Above the door was a sign which read "A1 Best Roasted Meats". On each side were line illustrations of a duck and a flayed pig.

The three of them stepped back as they heard the door being unlocked. A stocky man with a cherubic face, dressed like a chef, stared at them, and looked at the bag on Uday's shoulder. He reached for the bag, but Uday pulled it away. "My daughter first."

The cherubic looking chef waved them in, locking the door behind them. He directed them to walk towards the refrigerators. The room was hot, as if a huge oven had opened towards them. It looked like a food factory. Uday rushed to Lavinia's side and stared at his daughter as she lay on a long, narrow steel table. He reached for his phone. Hands trembling, he tried to call an ambulance, but stopped to look at Lavinia, her dress torn and dirty.

"My ... my ... baby ..." Uday leant over Lavinia's body, holding her gently. "My little princess. Please ... please stay alive. You must get well." Pulling away and barely able to stand, Uday sobbed as he stroked Lavinia's face, streaked with blood. In the shadow of the dim blue light shining from the other end of the factory, he saw the bruises and the wounds. Her left eye was swollen shut and her ear was bleeding. Both sides of her face were slashed and she was bleeding from the back of her head, causing her mass of jet black corkscrew curls to clump in places. Her arms and legs were in various shades of black and blue, with blood still oozing from scrapes all over her limbs.

Uday called for an ambulance.

Ashwin took one look at Lavinia and rushed towards the chef. With his hands squeezing the chef's collar, Ashwin shoved him to the ground. The man crossed his arms over his face, protecting himself from the blows that rained on him. "Not me! I never do anything!"

Sayana grabbed his brother, who was now straddling the man and was about to hit him again. "She's alive. Dad has called an ambulance."

Ashwin stood up and looked down towards the man who was lying on his side, his arms shielding his face. "This fuck tried to kill Lavi!"

"No! Please, I tell you true. He say she already die, kill her, burn her. Also burn her clothes, her handbag. He leave kitchen, then I see she not die. I find her phone. I call you. Eh, I save her!"

Uday glanced at his daughter as he bellowed, "Burn Lavi? Who wanted such a violent end for such a gentle soul? Who?"

Sayana pulled the man up and told Ashwin he would speak to him in Mandarin. "You're not going to understand a word so just go help Dad with Lavi."

"I've called an ambulance, but we should also call the police.

He can't kill her now. We're here." Uday typed the first "9" on his phone.

"Hold it, Dad! Not yet."

"Look at her, Ashwin. The monsters, whoever they were, nearly killed her. Attempted murder. We need to call the police."

Ashwin took the phone from his father. "If Lavi is supposed to be dead, then we can't let the criminals behind this think she's alive. Involving the police at this stage could mean this story being splashed all over the papers. Her attackers would look for her and try to kill her again. That fellow said she was okay, so let's just call Dr Dubash."

"Too late. I've already called an ambulance. She needs to go to a hospital. I think you've been watching too many stupid crime shows. Call the police!"

Ashwin redialled the number and asked for the ambulance to be cancelled. "She's not as bad as we thought. We'll take her home and ask our GP to make a house call." He returned the phone to his father. "We'll need to go soon. You know what, Dad? Let's say the police catch whoever who did this. Do you think their punishment will be enough? No, Dad, it won't."

Uday had never seen such fury in anyone's eyes. "You want vengeance. I want justice. We cannot take the law into our own hands, Ashwin."

Ashwin stared at his sister's limp body, the bruises and wounds still raw. "The law, no matter how objective you think it is, will never grant us adequate justice for such brutality. We should not, but we must handle this ourselves. We will find out who did this, and we will make him pay. Whether you like it or not."

Uday, weary and distressed from the viciousness surrounding him, croaked, "What have you become, son?"

2

Four Months Earlier, October

It was in the middle of Dussehra. Uday Aurora was in Mumbai during the Hindu festival honouring Rama's victory over the demon, Ravana, when he received the call. Suresh Gupta, founder and Chief Executive Officer of Fortuna Global, had collapsed at dusk during a typical daily ritual—eating kebabs and drinking whisky in his office. He died before the ambulance arrived. Even before Uday was told the cause of death, he knew it had to be a heart attack. Suresh Gupta loved food, especially mutton and anything with cream. His favourite snack was *pakoras,* deep-fried to a golden brown, and his favourite drink was mango milkshake, which he often spiked with a generous dash of whisky. At sixty-four, Suresh Gupta was obese. But even then, no one had expected him to die of his first heart attack.

The next morning, the management team of India's biggest, and richest, privately-owned hospitality and property development company met at Fortuna Global's headquarters in downtown Mumbai. Standing outside Suresh Gupta's spacious office, the decaying buildings beyond the dust-lined windows partially obscured by yellowing venetian blinds, Uday thought of Suresh for all that he was. And all that he wasn't. Uday felt wistful and regretted not having made a bigger effort to wine and dine Suresh and his wife when they had visited Singapore recently for a brief vacation.

A young man in a khaki uniform and metal buttons, which made him look like a bus conductor, offered Uday tea and cake. Having lost the taste for cloying Indian cakes, Uday politely declined those in favour of a bottle of ice-cold soda water. In Singapore, he missed the daily ritual of someone serving employees their mid-morning and mid-afternoon snack and hot drink. Uday watched some of his colleagues helping themselves to two slices of cake, while the tea-boy poured drinks from flasks labelled "Kofee" and "Chai". This benefit was not a frill to his colleagues; it was a right they took for granted. At Uday's office in Singapore, one of the world's most expensive cities, it was a luxury he could not justify. His employees seemed sufficiently content with a simple coffee machine, tea from Sri Lanka and China, and a variety of biscuits, including Digestives and Oreos.

Uday scanned the room. The men spoke amongst themselves in hushed tones. In the years he had been away, Uday had become detached from the global team in Mumbai, while building strong ties with his Asia Pacific team in Singapore, Bangkok, Hong Kong, Shanghai and Sydney.

Shivram Gopinathan, the Chief Financial Officer, patted Uday's shoulder as he cleared his throat and stood up. "Gentlemen, there is a lot to do, so we should start. A moment of silence, please, for our dear departed founder."

The men bowed their heads, most of them closing their eyes. Except for Rajan Lakhiani, the Director of Human Resources, who picked up his piece of cake with his spindly fingers and took a large bite. The coarse chewing on his last mouthful signalled the end of the minute of silent contemplation.

Shivram Gopinathan broke the silence. "Ladies and

gentlemen, I'm going to get to the point. Mrs Gupta called me this morning and asked about appointing a CEO—"

Rajan shot out of his chair. "What's the rush? Suresh-ji's body—God bless his soul—hasn't turned fully into ash—"

"Shut up, Rajan! Don't be so disrespectful," said an elderly man sitting next to him. "Sit down and let Shivram continue."

"Let us not forget that Mrs Gupta's father started Fortuna, and together with Mr Gupta, built it into what it is today. Some of us have been around since the beginning and we remember those early years well." Shivram Gopinathan rubbed his short, thick beard which looked like tarred moss clinging to his smooth cocoa-coloured skin. "Until the moment comes when we must retire, I, for one, would like to serve a good leader. One who is worthy of taking over the reins from Mr Gupta." Shivram did not seem to be in a hurry to name Suresh Gupta's successor. He looked at everyone in the room, all eighteen of whom were in the upper rungs of management. Shivram seemed to relish keeping them in suspense. After a long pause, he clapped his hands and asked, "Who will be our new CEO, then?" He smiled as he glanced at Uday.

"I propose you, Shivram Gopinathan!" Joseph Pereira, the ebullient chief operating officer was known to be rather chummy with Shivram. "Fortuna is as successful, as rich, as it is because of your joint stewardship." He stood up, and with both hands outstretched and pointing towards Shivram, he continued, "I don't believe anyone here is as deserving as you, Shivram."

Several people clapped and cheered.

"Thank you, but I have no wish to be CEO. I was going to propose …" Shivram Gopinathan turned towards Uday and pointed his outstretched palm towards him.

The room was still. Uday took a deep breath and spoke softly, addressing no one in particular. "This is wrong. Just wrong." Uday shook his head slowly and placed a hand on the table. Turning to Shivram, he continued, "When we spoke yesterday, we agreed that Fortuna does not need a new CEO right away. Suresh had always said Aditya would succeed him. We must honour that wish."

"That was before Mrs Gupta called me. No one expected Mr Gupta to go so soon. Aditya isn't ready. Mrs Gupta said she gave this matter much consideration. This appointment comes from her, from the very top."

"This is Aditya's right. He's ready. I've worked with him. He spent a year at the office in Singapore. Give him the position and he'll grow into it. Trust me."

Shivram snorted, "Just because Aditya is Suresh's elder son does not make him the best successor. He's too young and inexperienced. Besides, there's nothing in writing. We need someone who can lead Fortuna for the next ten years at least."

"Aditya is exceptionally clever. Thirty-two is not that young these days, especially when inheriting a solid firm with a strong team of highly competent men and women. Many were younger when they became heads of great companies. Tech is famous for its young CEOs. I dare say Aditya is more capable than a number of you here. He is the rightful heir, and when the mourning period is over, he should be sworn in as CEO."

The others mumbled and grumbled.

In a voice laced with cordiality, Shivram said, "Uday, I respect your sense of honour, but these people are right. Aditya isn't ready to step into his late father's shoes yet. For the sake of the company, let's compromise. We'll have a caretaker CEO for five years, during which time, we'll groom Aditya to take over. *Theek hai?*"

Uday considered Shivram's proposal, but the others were already chanting, "U-day, U-day, Uuuu-day!"

Uday waved his hand to dismiss the suggestion. "No, no, no. I was planning to retire in a couple of years."

Shivram sat next to Uday. "You know you are the best man for the job. This is what Suresh would have wanted had he known he was going so soon. Five years, tops." Shivram waved his hand to quieten the enthusiastic men and women. Lowering his voice, he continued, "There's also that problem with Rohit—"

Uday leant back in his seat and frowned. He had always done his best to hide his intense dislike for Rohit. "What kind of problem?"

Shivram stroked his beard. "Rumours have swirled since his engagement to your daughter that Rohit plans to take over from his father. Probably expects that you'll stand behind him, being his future father-in-law. All the more reason you need to step into this role, to prevent Rohit from planting himself in Suresh's seat immediately."

Uday stared at Shivram. "Are you saying he's marrying Lavinia to get to the top in this company?"

"Not at all. I'm sure he loves Lavinia and is marrying her for all the right reasons. He's just being the opportunist he is, and always has been."

"Why didn't you tell me about these rumours? The engagement was months ago. They're due to marry in June next year."

"There didn't seem to be any point. What could any of us have done? It's not like we were expecting Suresh-ji to just drop dead … God bless his soul …"

Uday excused himself and walked down the narrow, musty corridor. He paused just before it opened to a space filled with men and women on their imitation Herman Miller chairs, facing computer screens propped on dull grey desks. Uday watched them with an unsettling mixture of joy, gratitude and loss. Like himself, many of them had been hired fresh out of university and were due for retirement in a few years. Suresh Gupta had taken good care of his employees, paying them well and advancing anyone who showed promise.

It had been more than thirty years since Uday had joined Fortuna, then housed in a decrepit old building near Colaba. He was an intern waiting to enter university on a Fortuna scholarship programme at Edinburgh University. Upon graduation, Uday returned to serve a six-year bond, starting as a management trainee. In those early years, Fortuna was barely making a profit. Sheer grit and hard work, along with generous bank loans, catapulted the company into the ranks of Mumbai's big corporate players within ten short years. Now, more than thirty years later, Fortuna was on the list of every respected business magazine featuring businesses in India.

Uday had always known Rohit to be smart and determined. He lacked the scruples for which his parents were known, but most people were willing to overlook Rohit's flaws by focussing on his charm and sense of humour. But Uday had felt devastated when Lavinia told him that she had been in love with Rohit for years, and that he had chosen to do his Master's in Singapore so they could be closer. Unable to bear the thought of Lavinia moving to Mumbai upon her marriage, Uday had promised Rohit a position at the Fortuna Asia Pacific office in Singapore. Rohit had willingly accepted the offer. Uday was not prepared to witness Fortuna's unravelling over a younger sibling's greed for power.

He returned to the conference room. Complete silence fell abruptly over everyone. He asked for a private discussion with Shivram and watched as the others sauntered out of the room, some eyeing him with suspicion.

He ran his hand along the cold stone in front of him, smiling.

"You remember that trip?" Shivram asked as he turned his chair to face Uday. "I couldn't go as it was too close to Eid."

Uday nodded. He had forgotten that Shivram had married a Muslim woman several months before the trip. "Just before I moved to Singapore. We were on our way to the animal sanctuary in Rajasthan to make a big donation. On a whim, Suresh insisted on stopping at Abu Road. This office was almost complete. Suresh had heard about Abu Black being Rajasthan's finest marble, and had asked for the most richly textured stone in deepest black, with dramatic splashes of white."

"Suresh always knew exactly what he wanted."

"And he always got what he wanted. No matter what the price. It took three hours of viewing countless slabs before he was satisfied with this. It was sheer torture in that desert heat and the weak Indian air-conditioning."

"I know you'd like to respect Suresh-ji's wishes but Aditya simply isn't ready. You must lead Fortuna. For now, at least."

"I can't live in Mumbai. It'll be hard to leave Singapore's efficiency behind. And greenery. Oh, and the very effective air-conditioning."

Shivram laughed. "Yes, yes … And the food—"

"Especially the food!"

"Mrs Gupta was expecting you to come up with this excuse." Shivram laughed. "Run the company from Singapore, then. We'll work out the details. Besides, there's a rumour you're planning to marry that woman from China. Tamara? She'd be miserable in India."

Uday laughed. He could not imagine Tamara Wang in Mumbai. The city's pavements were not designed for her killer heels.

3

A Saturday in October

As summoned, Uday's sons, their wives and his daughter, Lavinia, gathered around the ten-seater dining table for a late breakfast. Uday was drained from a week of Dussehra celebrations in Mumbai. His head was still throbbing and he did not want to see another Scotch or hear another Bollywood song for as long as he lived.

Ashwin, his son and eldest child, laughed as he handed his father a large mug of ice-cold sugar-cane juice, bought by their Indonesian cook that morning from a stall at Adam Road. "Sure, Dad! We'll see. You've said this before. There'll be a Scotch in your hand just a few days from now—"

Uday pressed his fingers against his temples and moved them in a circular motion. "Nope! No more Scotch. Ever!"

His daughter and youngest child, Lavinia, hugged her father. "Ashwin's probably right, Dad. Sounds like you had hell of a time in Mumbai."

Uday's second son, Sayana, raised his coffee to his father, "Once again, Dad, congrats! CEO of Fortuna Global. I'm so proud of you."

Uday loved these moments when the whole family got together. As long as Ashwin and Sayana were not quibbling, the five of them brought much mirth and joy to his home. Uday raised his mug and said, "Thank you. It's only for a few years. But you know what ..." Uday breathed in deeply and leant against his chair. Nodding slowly, he continued, "As much as I've done for Fortuna, as rich a life as Fortuna has given us, nothing matters more than all of you. Nothing!"

Lavinia shrieked "Me the most, Daddy! Because I'm your favouritest daughter!"

Ashwin laughed, "And our favouritest sister!"

Uday smiled and immersed himself in the affectionate atmosphere while the family teased each other and waited for Uday to tell them why they had to meet so urgently. His beloved late wife, Julie, would have been proud of their children— Ashwin, at twenty-seven, a rising star in foreign exchange trading at a Swiss bank and married to Angela, a beautiful financial analyst in a rival bank, pregnant with their first child; Sayana, at twenty-six, teaching English Literature at one of Singapore's elite schools, and recently married to Priyanka, a copywriter in an advertising agency; and Lavinia, their unexpected and most welcome gift, the light of her father's life. The twenty-two-year-old had recently graduated with a law degree and was engaged to Rohit Gupta, younger son of the late Suresh Gupta, founder of Fortuna Global. With the exception of Rohit, Uday could never have conjured up a more perfect family.

Uday tapped his teaspoon against the handle of his mug. "I am a very lucky man ..."

Ashwin and Sayana cheered while the women clapped.

"It's true! But there's just one thing—"

"A dog! Daddy, are we getting another dog? Please say yes. I really miss Coco."

Everyone laughed. "No, my princess. Not a dog. I'm going to get myself a wife."

Uday had not expected the response this evoked. He wasn't sure which was worse—silence so thick it smothered him, or the five faces so morose that he felt he was drowning in melancholy.

He spoke softly. "I see no one was expecting that. But it's not like Tamara is a secret."

Lavinia burst into tears. "She's horrible, Dad! I can't stand her. She's as fake as those designer clothes at Far East Plaza! I can't believe you're doing this! How could you?" Lavinia ran to her room.

Uday followed her, gesturing for his sons and their wives to wait for him.

"My princess, Tamara is really a lovely woman. You just need some time to get to know her. You'll see that she's good for me—"

"Don't you miss Mummy? Do you think she'd approve?"

Uday felt a stab right through his chest.

"Lavinia, my darling, I think of your mother every day. I see her in you and your brothers. But she is gone and while she will always live in my heart, I cannot physically have her with me, by my side. And yes, Lavi, your mother would approve. Before she left us, she had asked me not to wait too long to find a companion. I told her she would always be my companion, and you know what? She laughed! Yes, a soft laugh because she was so weak, but she told me I was being silly."

Lavinia, who was lying on her bed, sat up. "She said that? Really?"

Uday nodded. "I would never make up something like that."

"Why can't she be your mistress, like she's been all these years?"

"She can't possibly live here permanently on a tourist visa. My marrying her is the only way she can live here legally. Please,

Lavi. Try and understand. In time, you'll grow to like her. I'm sure of that."

Lavinia walked towards Uday and hugged him. "I cannot understand what you see in her, Dad. But if she makes you happy then, well … I suppose … I mean, who am I to rob you of a second chance at love?"

"Thank you, Lavi. It would be a problem if you object and refuse to accept our marriage."

"I suppose I could say the same about my engagement to Rohit. I know you don't like him, but he'll prove you wrong, Dad. You'll soon see he's the right one for me." Lavinia hugged Uday and kissed him all over his face before warning him, "You should check with Ashwin and Sayana. They hate her just as much, you know. Just because they don't live here doesn't mean they'll be very welcoming, Dad. They're here for dinner nearly every evening and living in the same condo, they'll see her a lot. Go, Dad, talk to them."

Uday returned to the living room with an expression-less Lavinia.

"Well, boys, Lavi has given me her blessing—"

"I wouldn't go that far, Dad!"

A chastened Uday continued, "Lavi did not give me her blessing but she withdrew her objection. I've been thinking of marrying Tamara for a while."

"We understand, Dad," said Ashwin. "We respect your wish to marry Tamara but please don't expect us to welcome her warmly into our lives. We'll be polite towards her. We will accept her as your new wife. She will be our stepmother but there will be no love for her. I hope you can understand that, Dad."

Uday noticed Sayana, Angela and Priyanka nodding slowly as Ashwin spoke.

Angela sidled up to Ashwin and said in a soft voice, "She'll expect more from me. I'm not sure I can keep up the pretence. I feel she expects me to be extra nice to her because we're both from China."

Ashwin wrapped his arms around Angela. "You'll just have to show her in your own gentle way that being from China does not make you her comrade. There'll be no reason for you to spend any time with her alone. You'll be fine."

"I think you're all being unduly pessimistic. Please, I beg you, all of you, give her a chance. Is that too much to ask?"

No one spoke.

"*Theek hai.* I'm sure this will all change as the weeks pass and you spend more time with Tamara. She will grow on you."

Uday decided against opening the bottle of vintage Krug, perfectly chilled specially for this occasion.

4

It had been four months since Tamara's husband, Richard Wilson, was kidnapped and murdered. Today, on his way to Shanghai to see Tamara, Uday thought back to the day when she had called him, begging him to transfer a million dollars to save her husband's life. But Uday was not about to save the life of a man who beat and publicly humiliated his wife and who assaulted anyone who so much as took a little long at the ATM or overtook him on the highway. It would be bad karma to intervene in the extension of an evil entity's life. Let destiny take its course. Besides, Uday knew Richard had much more than a million dollars stashed away somewhere.

No one knew for certain what Richard did for a living—import export, he claimed, but never offered a clue as to what the items were. No one knew for certain where Richard came from or even what his real name was; he had three different passports and spoke with an affected English accent, trying, and failing, to mask a Slavic one. Richard Wilson was an ordinary name for someone who needed to pretend to be English while travelling on a British passport in a country where no one knew one foreign accent from another.

Everyone knew Richard had money and Tamara would

know where to find it. Two days after Tamara had called Uday, Richard's body was found floating in the Huangpu River, with fractures at the base of his skull and a knife wound through his heart. The police questioned Tamara at length. Within days, three men were arrested. Neither the murder weapon nor the ransom money was recovered.

Uday had flown up to Shanghai to comfort Tamara. The poor woman was confused—she had paid the full ransom, finding eight hundred thousand dollars in Richard's safe, which she had to break into, and several hundred thousand in their joint bank account. Yet they murdered him. Tamara Wang was distraught at being left both widowed and penniless.

"You are hardly a pauper! You still have a few hundred thousand in the bank, Tamara. I'm sure you'll soon find more money turning up. He had lots. It's common knowledge. Plus, your apartment in Grand Summit must be worth two million dollars."

Tamara had wailed as she scrolled down the comments on the New China Woman website. "Look, Uday! They are saying all these wicked things about me! People always hated Richard and me. They're jealous, but now that he's dead, they hate me even more!" Tamara clicked on an old picture of herself in a swimsuit and translated the comments as she read them. "Tamara Wang, socialite and former beauty queen is now up for sale ... Tamara Wang should do penance by becoming a nun ..."

Uday slammed Tamara's laptop shut. "Stop it, Tamara! There's no need to torture yourself. There will always be people who say hurtful things, strangers with nothing better to do." Uday pulled her close and stroked her hair. "Richard is gone. His kidnappers got their million dollars. You should be safe enough, but I'll hire a full-time bodyguard for you. Just to be sure."

Tamara pulled away from Uday. "No. Please, no bodyguard. I ... I ... don't need the attention. I'll be fine. Truly. Don't worry."

"Alright then, no bodyguards. But I will take care of you and Charlie."

From then on, Uday sent Tamara a monthly allowance and spoke to her twice a day, every single day, to assure himself that she was safe.

Ever since he met Tamara, Uday had looked forward to his business trips to Shanghai. Except this was going to be a trip with a difference. This visit was going to change his life and he looked forward to making Tamara and her son, Charlie, part of his family.

Uday was repulsed by Tamara's first-born, a crude thirty-year-old woman named Sharon, conceived in an assault by Tamara's father's colleague, also a close family friend. While dismayed that Sharon had chosen to move to Singapore several years ago, Uday was glad that she had never bothered to contact him. All Uday knew was that Sharon had spent the past two years working as a chef at one of Singapore's top Chinese restaurant chains.

In Uday's plush hotel suite, Tamara admired the ring on her finger. Cuddling up to him, she whispered, "I've been waiting for this, Uday. Ever since Richard died."

"I've been waiting for this ever since I met you at that embassy ball in Beijing."

Tamara laughed and punched Uday's arm. "Liar! All you talked about was your wife. At first, I thought she'd dumped you. You sounded so smitten! I remember thinking she was so lucky to be loved like that."

"Ah, but right after that, I could not stop thinking of you. I arranged my schedules just so every few months I could spend at least a week in Shanghai. It was never for the love of this city, as you know."

Uday kissed Tamara. He could not take his eyes or his hands off her. After five years of yearning for the exquisite Tamara Wang to be by his side constantly, after five years of begging her to leave her violent husband, Madam Tamara Wang, the widow, was now free to be with him. His loneliness, best expressed in the saddest of songs and movies, was about to come to an end. "This calls for a toast to the new life ahead of us." Uday called room service for a bottle of Krug.

Tamara sashayed towards the window and rubbed her arms. Her tight, short-sleeved dress which ended just above her knees, accentuated a sculpted figure, toned from a daily regime with a personal trainer. Without looking at Uday, she said, "Uday, darling, we can't just move with Charlie. We'll need to take Aaron with us, too."

"The nurse? Why? Singapore has excellent medical facilities, including private nurses. World class! They can deal with Batten's Disease in Singapore. We don't need a nurse from Australia."

Turning on her heel to face him, Tamara said, "Aaron has looked after Charlie for the past five years. Richard hired him when he thought Charlie was going to die soon. You've seen how bad he has gotten since you first saw him after the diagnosis. He won't live much longer, Uday, Batten's Disease is always fatal. Charlie can barely move now and is completely blind. The doctor says a year at the most. He'll be gone before he turns sixteen. Please, I beg you, let Aaron take care of Charlie."

Uday paced the living room of his suite. He had never liked Aaron, ever since he met him when he first visited Tamara at her apartment soon after they had first met. Tamara and her husband had thrown a cocktail party and while Uday hardly spoke to either of them, he had noticed Aaron sidling up to Tamara whenever she approached Charlie's bedroom. Years later, when Uday visited Tamara days after Richard's murder, he caught Aaron leering at Tamara while she spoke to well-wishers. Uday was sickened by the thought of this reptilian pretender living under his roof.

"It's not as if a nurse from the Philippines can't provide the same, or even better, care. I'm sure Aaron is expensive. We could probably get three nurses on round-the-clock shifts for less. That's so much better for Charlie. I'd rather we hire someone who's already in Singapore. Besides, we might not get a visa for Aaron."

"I'm sure there are ways. So many people from China get visas quite easily. Western people too, I heard. We must at least try—"

"I don't like him. Not one bit. You shouldn't trust him, Tamara." Uday noticed his hands were trembling. He turned towards the window, wringing his hands.

"Why would you think that, Uday? You don't even know Aaron!"

"The couple of times I saw him, I noticed him behaving inappropriately—"

"Inappropriately? What do you mean? Surely you were imagining things?" Tamara's voice and demeanour suggested she was genuinely baffled.

"I mean, a nurse or employee simply does not behave like that with his employer. The way he looked at you, the way he cozied up to you ..." Uday hesitated before continuing; he wasn't entirely sure if what he was about to say was true, or merely his imagination. "What irked me was the moments he picked—he gave you that look when he knew I would notice. Like he wanted to tell me that there was something going on between you two—"

"Uday! How could you?"

Uday walked towards Tamara and took her hands in his. "I knew there was nothing from your side, but it made me wonder why he was playing these games. Sinister fellow. I really would not like him in my home, Tamara."

Tamara laughed as she leant forward to kiss Uday. "Uday, my darling, you must have been imagining things. Aaron likes men! He has a lover, an older Chinese man who lives in this block."

Uday tried to remember the details of that day. Aaron may well be gay, but those looks he gave Tamara, knowing Uday was watching, were hardly the tactics of a gay man.

Uday would have to do what he could to prevent Aaron moving to Singapore. "No, Tamara. I do not trust him. We don't need Aaron. We'll get the best nurses for Charlie in Singapore."

Tamara stroked Uday's face. "Charlie won't live for much longer, Uday. Aaron knows how to care for him. Please, Uday. Please?" Her eyes, artfully hued in shades of grey and blue and framed by eyelash extensions for which she spent two hours at the salon every month, bored into his. Her lips, brushed with the lightest tinge of shimmering pink, were close to his, and continued to beseech him, though she had stopped talking.

Tamara was the only woman Uday knew who could turn a plea into someone else's obligation.

While he could still taste the venom on the tip of his tongue, Uday managed to whisper, "OK, my beautiful Tamara, we'll ask Aaron to move to Singapore with us."

Uday could only hope that Aaron would turn down her request.

**

Uday and Tamara set their wedding date for March 2015. It was to be in Singapore. Tamara had consulted a feng shui master, who determined a date in July to be the most auspicious, based on their zodiac signs and birth dates and times. Unwilling to wait that long, she had consulted another feng shui master who conveniently arrived at a date in March. They agreed that Uday, born in December 1960, the Year of the Rat, and Tamara, born in August 1971, the Year of the Pig, would have their marriage solemnised on Wednesday, the eleventh of March.

"It's less than four months away, Tamara. That's all. We'll be living together until then. We'll need to get your tourist visa extended once, maybe twice, and after that, we'll apply for the long-term pass that lets you live and work in Singapore—"

"Work in Singapore? I haven't worked in twenty-five years, Uday!" Tamara threw up her hands in horror.

Uday laughed at the sight of her being horrified about having to work. "You are such a drama queen! No, my darling Tamara, you don't have to work. It's just that the pass lets you, if you choose to. You never know. You might want to start a little business of your own?"

Tamara perked up. "Yes! That's true! I never thought about that." Tamara walked towards Uday and threw her arms around him. "Oh Uday, you are so full of good ideas! I like the idea of being a Singapore citizen. Like famous stars Jet Li and Gong Li. They are originally from China, you know? I've heard that Jacky Chan, a big star even in Hollywood, is a permanent resident." Uday found Tamara's excitement endearing. But just as she had suddenly perked up a moment ago, Tamara went still. It was as if she had an internal switch to swing from one emotion to the next. Uday watched as she stared at the ceiling and placed a finger on her lip. Turning to Uday slowly, she whispered, "How about Charlie? And Aaron? Will they get long-stay visas, too? Charlie is too sick to keep travelling back and forth. He'll also need to fly first class, where they can fit a stretcher."

"We'll make arrangements for Charlie at my apartment. Sayana has cleared the last of his things from his room. We'll find Aaron a small place within an easy commute."

"No! He must stay with Charlie. He will share Charlie's room. Please, Uday, Charlie needs Aaron all the time. Unless … unless … you want me to sleep in Charlie's room every night?" Tamara hit his sweet spot with that pout. Those same rosebud lips with a tinge of glossy pink, which had captivated him when he first met her. "When Aaron goes out or takes a day off, I will take care of Charlie, or maybe we can have the servants do that."

Uday sighed. "Aaron will share Charlie's room, then. But I'll draw the line at him dining with us. He isn't family. He'll be an employee, so he'll have all his meals with our helpers and the driver in the kitchen. It's big and airconditioned."

Tamara sulked. "Okay."

"One more thing—we don't refer to Wati and Maribel as servants. Wati is our cook, and Maribel is our housekeeper. No one calls them servants."

"Okay." Tamara was still sulking. She hated being corrected. "Also, what about my flat? I don't want to sell it—"

"No, don't sell it. The market hasn't picked up. Rent it out—"

"No! I won't have strangers living in my home. All those beautiful paintings and furniture … I should just keep it. I don't need the money and I don't owe the banks anything. I'll get someone to clean it—vacuum clean the entire house, dust all the ornaments—when I visit every few months."

Uday had thought the rental from the flat could go towards paying for Charlie's upkeep, especially to pay for that wretched leech pretending to be a nurse. But rather than appear avaricious to Tamara, Uday ended the discussion about her home. After all, it was not a big hardship to afford Tamara and all her accompaniments.

"Alright then, Tamara. As you wish. Just remember, it could take a few years before you become a permanent resident, and another couple of years before you become a citizen. Make sure you don't even get a parking ticket, okay? You must be patient."

Uday remained hopeful that, at the last minute, Aaron would change his mind about moving to Singapore. Better still, that the immigration authorities might have something on him and not allow him in.

Within days of their arrival in Singapore, Tamara's cargo of shoes, handbags and clothes was delivered to Uday's apartment. With the reluctant assistance of Wati and Maribel, it took Tamara six hours to unpack, check the inventory and put away all the trappings of her well-earned reputation as Shanghai's most stylish socialite. Uday arranged for twenty evening gowns and several fur coats to be placed in climate-controlled storage. He had initially baulked at the cost of hiring space just to temporarily put away some of Tamara's clothes, until new wardrobes were built at the far end of his bedroom, but was almost immediately relieved when he realised that three months of storage would cost less than two Valentino gowns.

As much as he hated the term, Uday accepted the price he had to pay for his trophy wife.

He was attending a conference in London when he received a text message from Lavinia: "Call me when you can. Not urgent. Just need to chat."

Uday knew Lavinia well enough. "Not urgent" was a euphemism for "It's not life and death, Daddy, but it's super important and I really need to talk to you as soon as possible."

Excusing himself during a break, Uday called Lavinia. It was nearly seven in the evening.

"Daddy! How's London? Still your favourite city?"

"Yup. Still my favourite. What's up, my princess?"

"Oh Daddy! I know I shouldn't bother you with stupid things, but a new coffee table was delivered today, and she had the old one removed! Can you believe it? I saw it when I got back from work. When I asked her about it, she just shrugged and said the previous one was the ugliest table she had ever seen. I told her it was Mummy's favourite piece and she said, obviously she had bad taste then! And she laughed! Daddy, she's horrible! We need to get that table back!"

Uday took a deep breath. He shouldn't have left her with so much cash. It was meant for an emergency, especially if Charlie had to be hospitalised. Tamara was probably restless and maybe felt the need to start making his flat her home. Women did that, didn't they? Mark their territory? Uday never liked that table much anyway, but Lavinia was right. He had to get it back. It was the first piece of furniture he and Julie had bought when they moved to Singapore.

Rubbing his forehead as he tried to picture the strong-willed Tamara arguing with Lavinia, who had the patience of a saint, but was sometimes prone to bouts of petulance, Uday said softly, "Lavi, I'll speak to Tamara. The table is probably at some warehouse. Please don't say anything to her. No need for either of you to get all heated up over a piece of furniture."

"Daddy! How could you say that? It's not just *any* piece of furniture. Frankly, I don't like it that much, but Mummy loved it, so we have to keep it."

"You're right, princess. I'll call her during my lunch break in a couple of hours. See you soon, my darling!"

Two days later, Uday landed at Changi Airport to find Lavinia smiling and waving to him from the other side of the large glass windows in the arrival hall. She looked tiny in her Hello Kitty jumper, at least two sizes too big for her. Uday wished Lavinia would get over her obsession with a mouthless white Japanese cat wearing a red bow. He much preferred her pre-teen infatuation with Disney princesses.

As he waved back while waiting for his bags, Uday revived fond memories of times when his wife had brought their children to meet him at the airport, even after a short two-day trip by him to Dubai. Julie never saw him off at the airport because it made her sad, but she was always there to welcome him back. That delightful ritual always reminded him that his growing wealth and steadily rising position at Fortuna meant little compared to the joy of being a husband and father. That ritual which he longed for, especially after it came to an abrupt end when his wife was cruelly taken away from him. As the years passed, the children had gotten out of the habit of meeting him at the airport but had always made it a point to be home when he arrived, unless they were in school or at work, or tied up in some inescapable activity. Today, Lavinia did exactly as he had secretly wished for some years, but had been too afraid to expect.

Whizzing his trolley past the customs officers and the automatic doors, Uday virtually flew into Lavinia's arms.

"What have I done to deserve this, Lavi?"

"I just felt like it, Daddy. And guess what? I drove here all by myself!"

Uday stared at her in mock horror.

"Don't worry, Daddy. I borrowed Angela's car."

As they walked to the car park, Lavinia's exuberance seemed to fade with every few steps.

Slowing down, Uday said, "I'll drive, Lavi. Give me the keys."

Lavinia stopped, took Uday's hand and asked, "Why, Daddy? I'm a good driver, you've always said so yourself. Let me drive! Please?"

Why did women always pout? Worse, why did he always feel obliged to succumb to any request preceding a pout? With Lavinia it was for everything from ice-cream as a three-year-old to a Cinderella costume at seven, a puppy at eight, countless other things and experiences in her teens, and now this. To drive her daddy home. He should have been pleased. But all he felt was a heart bursting from the anxiety he sensed in his precious child.

Uday sighed. "Please, Lavinia. Don't argue with me. I'll drive, and you can give me a run-down on all that has happened in the past week."

Lavinia reached into her bag and handed him her keys, grinning. "Are you sure you want to know?"

Uday turned down the volume of the Taylor Swift song playing in the background. "Is there some other music? All these songs sound the same."

"Daddy, she's my favourite singer and her songs are the best!"

Uday laughed. "Your mother and I failed with you and your brothers when it comes to your taste in music. Switch it to radio, please, or turn it off."

Lavinia found a station playing some hits from the seventies. Uday smiled and nodded.

"Daddy, something bad happened this morning. Maribel ran away."

"What? Why? Was she in one of those moods again?" Uday slowed down, moved into the centre lane and stayed within the speed limit. Maribel had been with the family for twelve years and while she was efficient and competent, she was also temperamental and impatient. Maribel still saw Ashwin as the fifteen-year-old he was when she first arrived from the Philippines. To her, Lavinia was, at times, still a ten-year-old who needed a friend to play with, or a troubled teen who missed her beloved mother.

Maribel had been known to walk away in a huff and lock herself in the bedroom she shared with Wati. Uday and his family tolerated Maribel's erratic behaviour because she was honest, caring and kept the house spotless, an ability prized by Julie, who, Uday was convinced, went undiagnosed as borderline obsessive compulsive. But not once had Maribel ever threatened to leave.

Lavinia turned to look at her father, who kept his eyes fixed on the East Coast Parkway Road. "Why else, Daddy? Your darling Tamara woke up this morning and decided to pick a fight with Maribel. I was on my way out when I heard some yelling in the kitchen. As soon as I walked in, I heard Maribel saying something about not having to work with a wicked witch—I think there were some Tagalog vulgarities thrown in—that the only queen in that home will be her late madam. She meant Mummy, you know, and then she made the sign of the cross and said, "god bless your soul ma'am", and ran to her room. I really had to run as I was already late, so I called Maribel while I was on the train. She said she couldn't be at our home for another minute and was going to her sister's employer's home. She said she wants a transfer to another employer but only you could make the arrangements, so I promised her I'd talk to you."

Uday pursed his lips and cocked his head. "Maribel didn't say what triggered it?"

"I asked her. She didn't want to talk about it. I asked Wati when I got home this evening and after much coaxing, she said it might have been because Tamara asked—no, she told Maribel— to give her a full body massage. Can you imagine? Maribel, spa therapist. Ha!"

"Maybe Tamara was used to that in Shanghai and didn't realise it was not the norm here, to have helpers provide such services."

"I've heard some employers expect to be massaged by their helpers. Even the men. Disgusting people! Probably Tamara's friends amongst them. Tamara's a real dragon woman." Lavinia chuckled. "Madam Naga. That's what I once overheard Wati calling her. I like it. That's what I'm going to call Tamara from now on. Lol—"

"I wish you'd stop using that word. Seriously, why don't you just laugh out loud, instead of using an abbreviation without even making an effort to laugh? It's so silly, like so many of your millennial words."

Lavinia chuckled. "You sound like Sayana. I can imagine him saying the same thing to his students. Anyway, as I was saying, Tamara has had a few names, apparently, so this would be just another one on the list."

"What do you mean?"

"Didn't you know, Daddy? She had been a fan of Jimmy Choo shoes for a couple of years before reading in some fashion magazine about Tamara Mellon, a co-founder of the brand. Some friends had given her grief about her previous name, so she changed it to Tamara. Just like that. Apparently, people in China have Western names, usually taken from luxury brands or celebrities."

Uday knew about the practice of absurd names for men and women in China. It was becoming increasingly common in Singapore, too, but Uday had simply assumed Tamara was a name she had adopted while she was a student in the United States. "Did she say what her previous name was?"

"She didn't offer it, but I did ask. Are you ready for this,

Daddy?" Lavinia took her eyes off the road for a moment, to face Uday. With sheer delight, she said, "Her name was Lulu Wang. Can you imagine? Sounds like a stripper! And before that, she was Ariel because she loved The Little Mermaid. I laughed when she told me. I honestly didn't mean to be rude. She got up and went off to your room in a huff."

"Lavi, that really wasn't nice. I'm very disappointed. I hope you apologised."

"I did, when she finally emerged from your room, but she responded with a sulk. So, Madam Naga it will be."

"Please, Lavi. Don't speak of Tamara like that. There must be some misunderstanding. It isn't easy for her to leave her home and move here, first as a tourist without financial or immigration security, and then having to wait some months to get married."

5

Uday could barely wait to see Tamara, who undoubtedly was waiting with equal delight. He had found it especially pleasing to see Tamara in those years when he was in Shanghai on business trips. After a day of largely pointless meetings and even more pointless phone calls, the sheer joy of being greeted by his beautiful Chinese lover, waiting in his hotel room in her signature tight dress and high heels for their clandestine rendezvous, was like nothing he could describe. Not even when Uday had conversations with himself during his most private moments in the dead of night, when he was plagued by the guilt of loving someone else just a few years after Julie's death. To have her waiting for him in his home, to be able to see Tamara every day, was a reality he had never allowed himself to imagine. Not until Richard died.

This evening felt odd. Along with the elegant sway of her hips and the swing of her impossibly long limbs, Tamara wore a strange expression on her meticulously made-up face. The one where her skilfully tattooed eyebrows were arched just so, and her eyes drilled through his, while her lips curled. The look which supposedly said everything but nothing he could ever comprehend.

Uday hugged and kissed her while Lavinia skipped towards the kitchen. Tamara patted him on his back, like a mother welcoming back her teenage son from school, the son who did not like displays of affection. She then pulled away without looking at Uday and walked towards their bedroom.

Uday followed behind. What happened while he was away? Why did Lavinia not warn him? "Something wrong, Tamara?"

Tamara had her hands on her hips as she pirouetted to face Uday. "Yes! Something is wrong! Why didn't Lavi tell me she was picking you up at the airport? Why didn't she ask me to go along? So she can poison your mind? Tell you bad things about me? Hmmm?" Tamara's face was flushed and her nostrils were flaring. Her pale skin was turning dark pink.

"I don't know, Tamara. It was the first time in years. Maybe she didn't think to ask you simply because she's not used to having you around. I don't think she asked Angela or Priyanka. They're her sisters-in-law, she's very close to them, and they live in the next block! She probably just decided to pick me up on impulse. There's nothing to it, darling."

Tamara sat on the bed and sulked. "She hasn't made any effort to speak to me. In fact, I think she's going out of her way to avoid me. You know, in the five days you were gone, she only had dinner at home twice, both times in the kitchen. I think she deliberately came home late so she could have dinner with the servants. Aaron said the servants don't talk to him but they're very friendly with Lavi."

Uday ran his fingers through his hair. He was exhausted after his long flight from London. The last thing he wanted to do was discuss domestic issues. That had always been Julie's territory.

"Of course they're friendly with each other. They've lived with us for over a decade! Your reporter-nurse-friend can surely understand that?" Uday walked towards the door. "I'm going to pour myself a Scotch. Would you like one?"

Tamara nodded. "I need one."

"Let's watch an episode of Big Bang Theory. I could use a few laughs. Then we'll go to bed and discuss Maribel tomorrow."

"Maribel? Lavi told you about her! I was right, she met you at the airport to poison your mind!" Tamara threw herself on the bed.

Uday sat beside her and stroked her back. "Tamara, you must understand. Maribel has been with our family for a long time. Twelve years! Lavi was just ten and was on the verge of losing her mother."

Tamara turned around. Between sobs, she said, "I'm sorry Uday. So sorry. I understand your obligations towards Maribel. You're a good man. Find her another employer, but she mustn't come back!"

Frowning and shaking his head, Uday asked, "Why? What did Maribel say or do to you that you feel she should not be allowed back?"

"Can you hear yourself, Uday? Listen to your tone. Look at the concern on your face! All that … not for me! For Maribel! A servant! She has such a hold on you! Can't you see it? Did your wife not see it?"

"Good grief, Tamara! I can only call this paranoia. When did you become like this? A few weeks in Singapore and you feel threatened by a domestic employee from the Philippines?" Uday stormed out of the room.

Uday's hand shook as he poured himself a Scotch. He had never known Tamara to feel threatened by anyone, least of all a housekeeper. Tamara was the most confident person he had ever met. There had been times when he wondered if it was even possible for someone so self-assured to make room in her life for another person. But not long after falling for her like a love-sick puppy, he learnt it was nothing but a carefully cultivated disguise. That cold, steely exterior was mere cladding for a terrified woman trapped in a dismal marriage. Tamara Wang was like a porcelain doll, safest when kept in a locked cabinet. Uday Aurora had never known any pleasure greater than taking that doll out to play, her fragility dissipating with every little stroke of her perfect body.

Uday took a generous gulp of his drink before he entered their room. Tamara had stopped sobbing. She sat up as soon as she saw him. Uday noticed the room looked different; Tamara had bought a new rug and a few cushions in deep shades of blue and green. He preferred the neutral colours Julie had picked earlier, but felt sure he would soon get used to being surrounded by azure and emerald.

"I'm sorry, Uday. I'm just not used to servants—"

"Tamara, for the last time, Wati is our cook and Maribel is our housekeeper. You may refer to them as helpers but never servants. The word went out nearly thirty years ago when the foreign domestic workers came in."

Tamara whipped out her phone from her handbag. After a few taps on the screen, she read out aloud, "Servant. A person who performs duties for others, especially a person employed in a house on domestic duties or as a personal attendant." She placed her phone by her side and with a look that betrayed her smugness, said, "Maribel and Wati are servants. They are not helpers. We pay them to work, not to help us."

Uday rolled his eyes and sighed. It was tiresome enough having to discuss the issue of domestic help. Discussing semantics made his head hurt. "Alright. Let's just call them maids. Commonly used term preferred by agents, employers and migrant welfare organisations. Okay?"

Tamara nodded. "Can we just get another maid? Maybe it's best that I do the interviews? I'm the one who has to deal with her eventually."

Uday shrugged. He had no desire to get involved in the employment of domestic help. "Sure. What about Wati? Are you planning to fire her?"

"Uday, I'm not a witch!" Tamara spoke softly through her pout. "I'm sorry about Maribel. I didn't fire her. She left. I know Lavi is upset—"

"Not just Lavi. The boys will be equally upset. They were all very fond of her. Try and understand if they're not exactly warm towards you for the next few days." Uday looked away. Or weeks. Possibly months. "I'll speak to Maribel tomorrow. See if I can help her find a suitable employer. I'll sort something out. Right now, I'd like some sleep."

6

New Year's Day

The phone vibrated and rang at the same time on his bedside table. Uday looked at the phone screen. It was nearly 6am, and the caller was Shivram Gopinathan. Uday made a mental note to change the annoying ring tone, one of Lavinia's recent pranks, before answering the phone. Being woken up to the strains of a young pop starlet repeating "shake, shake, shake" was too much to bear at any hour.

"Damn it, Shivram, it's six in the morning!" Uday was not sure why his head felt like someone was pounding it against the wall.

"And happy New Year to you, too, Uday-ji!"

Uday sat up, and remembered returning from Ashwin's home long past midnight, having sung the obligatory Auld Lang Syne, toasting guests with free-flowing champagne and pulling several party poppers. "Yes, of course, happy New Year, Shivram. I'm sorry. I only got home a few hours ago. What's up?"

"I think you need to come to Mumbai. Today if you can. The boys are fighting. And you're an enemy now, about to be unseated, if that's possible."

Uday massaged his forehead with his left hand. "What? How did I become an enemy?"

"Rohit feels he is more suitably qualified than you or Aditya. He is doing all he can to replace you. There will be war between the brothers tomorrow. Mrs Gupta is more than capable of quelling this little revolt, but I think she wants her sons to sort this out themselves. And clearly, they can't, so she wants you to be the fire-fighter."

Uday's head felt as if it was being bashed through a wall.

"Just get the earliest flight. I'll book a conference room at the hotel. Please convey my apologies to Tamara."

"She's back in Shanghai. Visa run. Her son got an extension because of his condition. The nurse managed to get an extension quite easily. But Tamara didn't. Back next week. By the way, why can't we meet at the office?"

"Public holiday, no aircon in the building. Important detail, I'm sure you'll agree."

Both men laughed.

Shivram Gopinathan was waiting in the lobby. While walking with Uday towards the reception desk, Shivram confessed, "I wanted some time alone with you before the meeting. Aditya's cool, but Rohit ... Rohit seems hell-bent on taking over. Today. Something to do with the start of everything new and the stars being in alignment. He's gone completely nuts, I tell you!"

Uday shook his head. "My future son-in-law."

The two men spoke in Uday's suite. It was dreary outside. As there wasn't even a sliver of sunshine breaking through the clouds, no light to lift his spirits, Uday fixed himself a Scotch from the mini bar. Shivram opted for ginger ale.

"Tell me everything from the beginning. But before that, did the boys actually have the annual New Year's Eve party at their house? So soon after Suresh's death?"

"Yes. We thought it was disrespectful. Some of us discussed it and decided not to go, but Mrs Gupta heard about our concerns and insisted we continue the tradition. She said it was what Suresh would have wanted. So, we dispensed with the usual mourning rituals and went to the party. Just after midnight, Rohit grabbed a mike from one of the live singers they had hired and announced that this was going to be the Year of Rohit's Fortuna Global. Started thumping his chest and throwing around names I'd never heard of except for Jobs, Gates and Zuckerberg. Repeated those names a few decibels higher and said they were all leaders when they were still in their early twenties. Rohit insisted he was just as capable, and he would prove it. More chest-thumping. Dead silence in the hall.

"Aditya tried to get him off the stage, thinking he was drunk, but Rohit fought him off and Aditya stormed off. Rohit only stopped when Mrs Gupta went up to him and whispered in his ear. No one knows what she said, but Mrs Gupta was smiling while Rohit scowled as he made his exit. Just before he left the room, he came up to me and in a cold voice said, "Gopinathan, call Uday. Tell him to be here tomorrow."

Shivram paused to take a sip of his ginger ale. I yelled after him, "You think the CEO is going to fly here straightaway just because you asked him to?" And then like any thug in a B-grade Bollywood movie, he swaggered towards me, patted my chest, and said, "Yes. Because you'll see to it." I tell you, Uday, never in my life had I ever felt so scared, not even when my grandfather came after me with a whip. But that look, that voice … I never thought that child who used to run along our corridors and who helped himself to our stationery would turn out to be so vicious. Luckily my family had left an hour earlier. I was too ashamed to tell them that I felt threatened by a twenty-eight-year old spoilt brat."

"This could have waited a day, even a week. To start a meeting at 4pm on New Year's Day is thoughtless and insane. Goes against everything we stand for."

"I agree, but Rohit … Rohit …"

Everyone knew what Rohit was capable of. He was predisposed to violence, and for years had been protected by his mother, who made excuses for her son's behaviour. Rohit, his mother's golden boy, was always jealous of his older brother, Aditya, who was everyone's golden boy. There was a rumour, long believed to be true, that as a teenager, Rohit had lured a neighbour's puppy and strangled it to spite the neighbour's daughter, for talking to Aditya while spurning Rohit's advances. The puppy was found outside the neighbour's door with slashes all over its small body, nearly decapitated. Aditya, believing Rohit was vindictive enough to commit such an evil act, avoided speaking to the girl and her family. There was never any proof to link Rohit to the cruelty, but years later, while he was away in university, the girl's mother said that Aditya had secretly apologised to the family and resumed his friendship with the girl.

Uday paced the living room, aware of the stillness. He caught a glimpse of himself in the mirror. Pausing to absorb the image staring back, Uday wondered when he began looking older than his age. At fifty-five, his hair was completely white and thinning at the top. The dark circles under his eyes—common in brown skin—had worsened over the past year; he now looked like a racoon. Those lines along his forehead and the crevices running down by the sides from his nose to his lips … they must have appeared overnight.

"Quite unlike you to admire yourself in the mirror, Uday."

"I was wondering what happened to me. When did I begin to age, and so rapidly too?"

"We're all getting older, Uday. At least you're fit. You must be the only one in management without a pot belly."

"You're too kind." Uday patted his abdomen. "It's there, not as bad as many others we know, but this could be better. I need more time at the gym."

"Yes, yes, we all know how diligent you are about exercising. But the only people who seem to use the gym on the third floor are the young ones, those below thirty."

"Discipline, Shivram. That's all it is." A little vanity, too. Uday had seen too many successful, wealthy people morph into large men and women who could only waddle into and out of the fancy restaurants they frequented. He had sworn to exercise regularly and watch his diet, so that by the time he was fifty, his body would still be healthy and young. At nearly 1.9 metres tall, Uday had to be extra careful to maintain his relatively lean frame. He had done a good job but had neglected his face.

Shivram patted his paunch. "Too late for me. I'd rather buy bigger clothes than exercise."

An ice cube clinked as it melted and plopped, along with a few other cubes, further down Shivram's long, thick glass. Uday sat at the desk and turned the chair around to face the Arabian Sea, the water choppy and the sky every shade of grey. There was something ominous about having such bleak weather to ring in the new year, that celebration being one of the indelible vestiges of their colonial past.

In the two months he had been at the helm, Uday did not feel as if his leadership had made a big difference. Being based in Singapore when the company's pulse was in Mumbai had detached him from his team. He spoke to them every day, usually at noon, which was 9.30am in Mumbai. Sometimes twice a day. At times even more frequently, for up to an hour, especially when there was a problem. Like a few days ago, when an owner of one of their hotels in England was considering signing on with an American management company. Uday had to renegotiate a new deal two years before the contract was due to expire. Or a few months earlier, when work on a project on the outskirts of Mumbai had stalled because a few disgruntled workers had taken a supervisor hostage. Uday had to approve an immediate increase in wages and better dormitory facilities, including Wi-Fi and television. Other than him lending his authority to the negotiations, there was nothing that the management committee could not have handled.

He had an exceptional team in Mumbai—smart, driven and hardworking. They shared their founder's vision of making Fortuna Global one of India's most respected companies, and amongst the top ten employers to work for, in a list dominated by multinational companies. As the people in Singapore would say, Rohit Gupta could go fly a kite. Uday was not going to be cowed by the prodigal son of a man he had admired and loved. He would never allow the memory and legacy of Suresh Gupta to be dishonoured by a whiny and delusional young man.

Shivram walked towards the window, carrying his nearly empty glass, drenched from condensation. "Penny for your thoughts, Uday?"

"Haven't heard that phrase in ages!" Uday rubbed his chin and smiled. "I know exactly what must be done. Leave it with me." He waved his finger at Shivram. "I know that look on your face. You're afraid I might say or do something impulsive. Don't you trust me?"

Shivram tried to suppress a snicker. "You know I do, Uday-ji. Completely."

The members of the management committee were all seated

and chatting when Uday and Shivram walked into the conference room. Minutes later, Aditya walked in.

"I am so sorry to drag you here like this today, of all days. Especially having Mr Aurora fly over from Singapore. I don't know what has come over my brother, but it needs to be sorted out now."

Uday patted Aditya's shoulder as he took his seat. "We'll do what we have to do."

One of the directors snorted. "He'll probably keep us waiting, just to try and show us he's the boss."

Aditya rolled his eyes. "He's capable of that, yes. Don't bother calling him. He'll enjoy making you wait a little longer. He's a twisted fuck."

The room went still. They were used to hearing the f-word, often using it themselves, but never in the presence of older people, and certainly not in front of the big boss.

Uday took a deep breath and said, "Let's just wait. Would someone please order some snacks and drinks?"

It was over an hour before Rohit strolled into the room, his face as morose as the weather. In sharp contrast was the woman who walked in just behind him—his mother—a slightly overweight, elegant woman with a ready smile for everyone.

The men stood up. "*Namaste,* Mrs Gupta," said Uday, followed by a group echo. Aditya went over and kissed his mother.

"Sit, please sit … this isn't the army! I'm here as an observer and, as you can see, Rohit does not like it." Turning to Uday, Mrs Gupta asked, "Uday, it's alright for me to be here, no? As my late husband's widow, and this being a private company, I'd just like to make sure today does not spell the beginning of the end for Fortuna."

Uday, slightly startled, replied, "Of course, Mrs Gupta.

You're welcome to sit in on this meeting. Let's begin. Who's taking notes?"

Everyone looked at each other. Shivram responded, "We'll record the meeting for now and I'll get my secretary to type out the minutes tomorrow."

Uday began, "Rohit, could you tell us what led to the drama that played out at your house in the early hours of this morning?"

All eyes were on Rohit, who was staring at his twiddling thumbs. Without any warning, he stood up, banged on the table, and in a raised voice, said. "Everyone knows that I'm the best man for the job! You can't disqualify me just because I'm younger than him," Rohit stretched out his arm, at the end of which was a pointed finger, with such force, Uday thought both the finger and arm might come apart, propel themselves towards Aditya and go right through his face.

Aditya said softly, "Go ahead, Rohit. Do what you do best. Fight. Show everyone in this room that you have what it takes to lead an organisation our grandfather and parents built. Show them how much you deserve their respect." Aditya turned to face Uday. "Uncle, I have known for years that my father wanted me to take over the company upon his death or retirement, whichever came first. No one expected him to go so quickly. I think the people here were right to put you in charge. I hope you will resolve this and stay in charge. I can wait for five years."

"Because you're a pussy! You don't have what it takes to be a leader and you know it. You're stalling just to prevent me from getting what I deserve. Papa always believed in meritocracy. He always said I was the clever one." Rohit addressed the men sitting at the table. "Aditya was six or seven when Papa talked about him taking over. He could not have meant it then, or at least, later on, he was allowed to change his mind."

The rest whispered amongst themselves. Uday glanced at Mrs Gupta, who smirked as she tilted her head towards Rohit. Uday had always believed that she would stand by her favourite son no matter what, but today he wasn't entirely sure. Uday's heart ached to be reminded that in their teens, his own sons had stopped sharing the closeness they had as children.

At least they both turned out to be good men. He was relieved that, even though his older son, Ashwin, had his moments, neither of his boys possessed the innate hooliganism so evident in Rohit.

Uday raised his hand and asked for silence. "Rohit, you might be the only person in this room who believes your father wanted you to succeed him. As far as all of us are aware, the plan all along was for Aditya to take over."

"Did Aditya study in America? In England? Business schools in Wharton and Oxford? Was he ever educated abroad? No. Just a bachelor's degree from an Indian University. I, on the other hand—"

Suddenly Mrs Gupta got to her feet, put her hands on her hips, and with the eloquence for which she was known, said in a cold voice, "Aditya was a star student and all-rounder throughout school. Delhi University gave him an excellent education and he graduated with a first-class degree in economics. You, Rohit Gupta, were kicked out of various schools since you were fourteen. Got into a second-rate college in America because your father paid for a new library and music hall, and never completed your master's degree despite going to four different schools."

Mrs Gupta strutted in her stilettos towards Rohit, twirling her coiffured curls with her perfectly manicured fingers. "Let me refresh your memory. You didn't go to Wharton. It was Penn State. It wasn't Oxford. You went to Oxford Brookes. And in

Singapore, we got you a flat and you took a distance learning course because you couldn't get into any of the universities." Mrs Gupta stroked Rohit's face. "My beloved son, as your mother, I will always love you. But I'll be damned if I let you run this company to the ground with your hubris."

Rohit glared at his mother. "Mummy! How could you? This is the ultimate betrayal!"

His mother lit a cigarette and said, "Son, the ultimate betrayal would be for me to watch while you destroy this company. Anyway, like I said, I'm just an observer who wanted to set the record straight because I could. Uday's in charge."

Uday wanted to laugh at the sight of Rohit, who looked as if he had lost a game he was set up to win. At the same time, Uday felt like slapping the twit for wasting everyone's time on a public holiday, time that they should all have been spending with their families.

Rohit crossed his arms as he spoke. "No! Daddy meant for me to be the next generation leader. Fortuna needs a roaring tiger, not a kitten like Aditya."

"*Bas,* enough!" Mrs Gupta raised her hand. "Stop it. These people didn't come here to listen to you two squabbling." Addressing Uday, Mrs Gupta said, "You're the CEO. Make this problem go away. And you, Rohit. Just shut up and listen."

"Oh, Mrs Gupta, it is very simple. After several hours of reflection on the plane, I've decided that Aditya is ready. What he lacks in experience, he more than makes up for in wisdom and maturity far beyond his years."

Aditya sat still, his hand stretched out in front of him, grasping the edge of the table. Could he not hear the others chanting his name, the way they chanted Uday's name just months earlier? He seemed to be in a trance.

Uday walked up to him and placed a hand on his shoulder. Aditya flinched. "Congratulations, Aditya. We'll get this all sorted out officially over the next few months."

As the men got up to leave the room, Rohit spoke in a raised voice, "Uday Aurora! You'd better watch out. For a start, I'm breaking my engagement to your daughter. Who wants a weakling like you for a father-in-law? Tell her, will you?" As he left the room, Rohit shrieked and whooped, the sounds meant to express scorn rather than a cheer. "This isn't over, Uday Aurora!"

Uday yawned. "I'm going to catch the late-night flight. There's no need for me to stay until tomorrow. We'll sort things out over the phone. Or Skype. Papers that need to be signed can be sent by courier."

"How blessed you are to be able to retire so young."

Uday grinned. "Fifty-five isn't that young. Almost our parents' age when they retired." Turning serious within seconds, he continued, "By the way, I don't see my circumstances as a blessing. That suggests divine intervention. I got lucky, that's all—"

"Supremely lucky! Getting into and out of Singapore's property market at just the right time. As much as three hundred percent in profits within six or seven years for three houses. Millions were made, I heard. Julie's inheritance before she died—"

Uday raised his hand. "That's enough, Shivram. Have you nothing better to do than to track the sales of my properties?" Uday made no effort to conceal his annoyance. Narrowing his eyes, he asked, "I have no idea how you even knew those investment homes were up for sale, and to know so much, I can only suppose that you paid for a subscription on a real estate website, just to see what my properties were bought and sold for. Did you?"

Shivram looked away. "I'm sorry. I got carried away. Everyone knows you did well with your investments and we are delighted." Shivram faced Uday and extended his hand. "I genuinely wish you all the best, Uday."

The two men stood in the lobby while waiting for Shivram's driver. The pianist played a piece Uday recognised but could not identify. Something from a movie. The soothing sound, amplified in the cavernous atrium, was in stark contrast to the raging sea just beyond the floor-to-ceiling windows.

"It will be hard for Lavinia, but you should be relieved, Uday. Imagine having Rohit as your son-in-law. Lavinia deserves so much better." Shivram was a reasonably sincere fellow, but his attempt at offering comfort was beginning to grate. "Just ignore what he said about this not being over. There's nothing he can do."

"Yes, Shivram. Thank you."

7

The Next Day

Nothing in Uday's career and parenthood could have prepared him for the moment when he had to face his daughter to break the news of her broken engagement to her. Much worse, that he was the cause of it. What if she never forgave him for destroying her future with the boy she had been determined to marry ever since she was twelve years old? Lavinia had lost her heart to Rohit when, during a summer vacation in Mumbai, he taught her how to play chess and introduced her to Coldplay by giving her two compact discs.

Uday boarded the flight and prepared to lose himself in movies while trying to forget the arduous task of bearing bad news several hours later.

On arrival, he let himself into his apartment. It was just after 9am. No one was at home except Wati and Conchita, the new housekeeper.

Days after Maribel had left, Uday had tried to convince Lavinia that Tamara should have a say in selecting their latest domestic helper.

"No, Daddy! She would choose the dumbest one, the inexperienced scaredy cat fresh from a village in Java, just so she can bully her. I'll rope in Angela and Pri to help with the interviews. Leave things to us, Daddy."

"Maybe you could, at least, let her meet the shortlisted candidates before you pick one?" Uday could not bear another episode of Tamara accusing Lavinia of plotting against her. "Please, Lavi. You'll get the final say. Just let Tamara feel that her opinion matters—"

"Her opinion doesn't matter, Daddy! Why should it? Maribel is gone because of her! The last thing we need is for Wati to go and then we'll start a never-ending rotation of helpers."

Uday knew when Lavinia was at the point of a frenzied argument, which would only lead to tears. "All yours then, Lavinia. But make sure Angela and Pri get involved. They'll inject some objectivity into your selection process."

Lavinia and her sisters-in-law picked Maribel's replacement after interviewing nearly twenty candidates. Lavinia decided that Conchita had the right balance of arrogance and defiance to manage Tamara and enough pride to keep the house immaculate, and the right balance of humility to take instructions from Uday and his family. Both Angela and Priyanka agreed that with twenty years of experience and three different employers, Conchita was by far the best choice.

His phone rang. It was Ashwin.

"That was probably the quickest trip you've ever made to India, Dad. Was the problem resolved? Did you put Rohit in his place?"

Uday was in no mood for a discussion. "All settled. Let's all have dinner here tonight. I'll call Sayana." Wati brought him some tea and fried eggs with bacon. "Breakfast is here. Must go." From where Uday sat, he could see Lavinia's half-finished book on the coffee table, next to Scrabble, her favourite board game. She must have had friends over last night.

"One more thing. I'd like us to meet at your place before

dinner. It's quite urgent. I need your advice. I'll ask Sayana to join us." With that weird nurse around, Uday preferred private conversations to be held outside his home. Uday had caught Aaron hanging around outside Charlie's room on the pretext of looking for something while clearly doing nothing, most likely to listen in on conversations.

"Sure. Bye, Dad. Enjoy your breakfast. Get some sleep."

Lavinia knew as soon as she walked into Ashwin's apartment that something was wrong. She sat on an armchair, dispensing with the usual hugs and kisses—a family ritual for as long as they could remember, as they left the house and when they returned home. Uday walked towards her and kissed her on the forehead. "Something bad happened. I know those looks. Exactly like when you told me about Mama's cancer when I came home from school that day."

Ashwin spoke. "It's Rohit—"

Lavi clasped her mouth. "Rohit? Something happened to my beloved Rohit?"

Uday sat on the arm of Lavinia's chair and put his arm around her. "Princess, nothing has happened to him."

"Not yet, anyway," growled Ashwin.

Uday glared at Ashwin before turning Lavinia's face towards him, "Lavi, my Princess, Rohit has called off the engagement and—"

"And doesn't have the decency to tell you so himself. Be glad, Lavi. This is a blessing!" Sayana was kneeling in front of his sister. "Rohit wanted to be CEO. Daddy gave up his position to keep the peace in Fortuna, to respect Suresh Uncle's wishes. Aditya is the new CEO, and for that Rohit has decided not to marry you. What a spiteful creature! Punishing his kind and beautiful fiancée because her father did the right thing."

Lavinia looked at her father. "Is this true, Daddy? Rohit called it off because of you?"

Ashwin took his sister's hands and said, "Rohit called it off because he wanted to spite Dad for handing the reins to Aditya. Shows what a spoilt, vengeful brat he is. Lavi, you deserve better."

Lavinia grabbed the cushion behind her, held it on her lap and leant back on the large armchair. She stared at the cushion, tracing the random patterns with her finger. Everyone remained silent. Uday's back was beginning to ache. He kissed her before going back to his seat. Lavinia took a deep breath. "Just before the engagement, I spoke to … I dreamt Mama and I were talking to each other. He's not the one for you, she said. I told Mama that people don't like him because they don't know him. She said it was I who didn't know him. I should've listened to Mama." Lavinia wept softly. Priyanka handed her a handkerchief and hugged her. "I … I had half a mind to call it off but all I could think of was how much I loved Rohit, how much I wanted to be with him and … that Mama didn't really know him."

Ashwin said, "Frankly, Lavi, no one liked him. We all tried to talk you out of it—not very hard, admittedly—but you were beyond reason."

Lavina wiped her face. "Mama is probably waving her finger at me, saying, 'I told you so!'"

Uday shook his head. "Mama's not doing that, Lavi. She's feeling your sadness."

Lavinia hugged the cushion before placing it behind her. "I need to be alone. I'll see you at dinner."

As Lavinia walked towards the door, Priyanka sprinted to her side and grabbed her hand.

"We're all here for you. Always."

"Pity not your sister-in-law, Pri. I've been dumped but not destroyed."

Priyanka held Lavinia's face in both her hands and said, "You have not been dumped. You have been released. The greatest gift from that scoundrel is your freedom."

Angela yelled, "And that ring. Let's not kid ourselves. A hundred thousand-dollar ring from Tiffany."

Uday said, "We'll return it. It's not hers to keep."

Lavinia removed her ring as she walked towards her father. "You're right, Daddy. I don't even want to keep it."

"You get to keep your dignity. You'll see that soon enough." Uday held his daughter for a long time before she pulled away and left.

8

A Few Days Later

The family sat down to a lavish Thai meal prepared by Conchita, even though her responsibility was mainly to clean the flat.

"Eight dishes! Quite a feat, Conchita," said Angela, serving Uday the red curry before dishing some on to Ashwin's plate.

"Used to it, Ma'am. Also, Wati help me do all the chopping and cleaning. Miss Lavi say the family like Thai food. But Ma'am Tamara and Mr Aaron don't like so I make all this when Ma'am Tamara go away. For Mr Aaron, I make chicken adobo. He say he like very much."

Sayana snorted, "Who cares what he likes? He's lucky he gets three square meals a day."

Priyanka placed her hand on his arm and said, "Hush! He'll hear you."

Conchita chirped, "He go out, Ma'am. He say he come home around ten. Wati and I help to check on Charlie. Today he little bit sick but now alright. Sleeping well."

"Aaron should go out more often. Every evening would be nice," mumbled Sayana.

Ashwin raised his hand towards his brother. "High five!" Uday smiled. It warmed his heart to see his sons agree on something, anything, even if it was only over their intense dislike for a despicable creature in their midst.

Every time Aaron was mentioned, there was a strange reaction at the table, alternating between a hush and visible discomfort. There was something going on with Aaron, but no one was telling him. Uday decided he would ask Sayana later. He was glad to see that Lavinia was reticent, but less sullen. He was hopeful that she would soon return to her chirpy, vivacious self. Rohit Gupta did not deserve Lavinia's despair.

Sitting at the round ten-seater table with his sons and their wives, and with Lavinia by his side, Uday was keen to provide the third instalment of events during his Mumbai visit. The news about Aditya taking over was well-received. The one about Rohit had been the most difficult news to break, but Lavinia seemed to have found a silver lining. Watching the family in good spirits again, and trying to whip up much needed mirth for Lavinia, Uday decided to save that piece of news for another day. Let them believe their assumption that he had simply returned to his previous position.

By the time Wati cleared the table for dessert, Lavinia seemed more light-hearted. The family's confessions of how they really felt about Rohit, and the warning in her dream by her mother, must have weighed heavily on her during her few hours of contemplation holed up in her room.

Ashwin raised his glass. "To Dad, welcome back to where you were before Suresh Uncle passed away. You were so much happier then."

Sayana laughed. "Of course! Tamara was still living in Shanghai at that time!"

Uday raised his hand. "Sayana, Please. I know you loathe her and I respect your loyalty to your mother, but please, young man, have the decency to keep those feelings to yourself. You have a beautiful wife and a future full of promise and delight. Let me enjoy what's left of my years."

No one spoke. The sound of spoons gathering the last of the pudding smeared around their bone china plates pierced the air.

"Sorry, Dad."

Lavinia, her straightened hair drooping over the sides of her face, stroked the handle of her spoon and spoke to no one in particular. "I think she's having an affair with that creep."

Uday roared. "Aaron?" He looked towards the kitchen and lowered his voice. "What a thing to say, Lavi! If you lot think I'll change my mind about marrying Tamara just because of your unfavourable opinion, then be prepared for a huge disappointment." Uday paused and gulp-emptied his recently filled glass of wine. "Besides, Aaron is a card-carrying, flag-bearing member of Pink Dot. Like your good friend, that dog groomer."

"Aaron is not gay, Daddy! I think it's all an act," insisted Lavinia. "My friend is very real, though. Love him to bits. But Aaron is devious, Daddy! And he is Tamara's lover. I've caught them looking at each other that way."

Uday did not expect his children to readily enfold Tamara in their love and warmth, but neither did he expect such loathing. Lavinia was letting her imagination get the better of her. He needed to be patient and more tolerant of his children's views, especially Lavinia's. She had suffered the most from her mother's death and remained fiercely loyal.

Uday took a sip of wine. "I'll keep a close watch on Aaron."

"And Tamara!"

"Yes, Princess. And Tamara." There was no point in challenging Lavinia when she was convinced her perception was the truth.

After a long pause, Sayana, who was sitting directly across the table from Uday, spoke. "Dad, does this mean you've been demoted and have to take a pay cut now that you're no longer CEO?" Curiosity was bursting through his eyes.

So much for saving the news for another day. A direct question deserved a direct answer.

"Much more than a demotion and even much more than a pay cut. I've resigned."

The gasp was audible even in the kitchen. "What happened? Everything okay?" asked Wati, as she popped her head through the door.

"Yes, Wati," said Uday. "We're done. You may clear the table." As Wati went back into the kitchen for the tray, Uday said, "Aaron will probably be back soon, and I don't want him eavesdropping. Let's go to Ashwin's."

Sayana glared at Ashwin as he addressed his father. "Why not my place? We're always going to Ashwin's."

"Because Angela is pregnant, and she has the option to go and lie down in her room if she so pleases. And no, we're not always going to Ashwin's. It's not a competition, Sayana."

Uday grabbed his keys and led the family out of the apartment and to Ashwin's, a five-minute walk away. He could not remember when Sayana had begun to feel compelled to outdo Ashwin in everything, from sports to academics. He watched his sons as they held their wives' hands. As Sayana quickened his pace to be in front of Ashwin, Uday could not help but believe that Ashwin had held himself back at school just so Sayana could feel he did better.

Even during Ashwin's attempts to grow a beard or moustache— it was sparse, at best—and even when he got himself a bad haircut, Ashwin was the better looking of the two. Although his skin was as dark as Uday's, Ashwin had inherited his mother's fine features—a straight, sharp nose, thin lips and light brown eyes, while Sayana, with much fairer skin, fuller features, and an overbite that was not fixed due to his rejecting braces in his teens, looked more like Uday's father. For all his roughness at times, Ashwin was the most loving, obliging and loyal person Uday knew.

While Uday helped himself to a Scotch and soda, the rest of the family made themselves comfortable in Ashwin's modest home. It was not quite half the size of Uday's, but spacious enough for a small family and a live-in nanny, if Angela decided to return to work after giving birth. The apartment, built in the mid-eighties, had had some cosmetic updates but was never fully renovated, making it look worn and dated. Sayana's flat was in a similar condition. But after Uday made the down payment on the flats for both his sons, the mortgage was all that Ashwin and Sayana could afford, while wishing to live close to the family. Uday was glad that both his sons inherited their mother's good taste when it came to decorating their homes.

Uday pulled out a chair from the dining table and placed it so he could face all five of his close family members.

"I've decided to retire."

Sayana leant forward. "But Dad, you're only fifty-five! Even in the civil service, retirement age is now sixty-two."

"I'm not going to stop working. I'll start a consultancy. The hospitality industry is in overdrive, and with all the connections I have, there'll be enough to keep me busy."

Ashwin seemed more receptive to the news. "And sufficiently compensated, I'm sure! You'll be making more while working less." Everyone laughed.

Angela chuckled as she pinched Lavinia. "Someone's got to pay for Lavi's shoes, right?"

"Well, yes, that's true. But seriously, an income will help while our investments aren't doing that well. Besides, I'd like to travel a little more, go away for a lot longer. Consulting lets me travel while paying for the expenses. Two months in Italy, for a start."

"Long honeymoon, then?" Angela winked.

"Delayed honeymoon. The six-month notice started on Monday. Won't be going until July."

Sayana grimaced. "So hot! The worst possible time to visit Italy. An antipodean holiday might be better. New Zealand … or South Africa!"

Uday nodded as he pictured a map of the Southern Hemisphere he had drawn as a secondary school student who hated geography. "Argentina. It takes forever and a day to get there, plus time to recover from such a long journey. Time is all I'll have to discover Buenos Aires, the Pampas and Patagonia." Uday cocked his head. "Come to think of it, Tamara would hate that. She'd love the city but not the countryside … Maybe I'll just have to wait until September to spend those two months in Italy."

"Or take me to Argentina in July!" Lavinia seemed more cheerful as the night wore on.

While everyone laughed, Uday noticed Ashwin staring at a book on the coffee table. It had been there for months. Ashwin certainly wasn't contemplating the typography or choice of imagery on the cover. "What's wrong, Ashwin?"

Angela nudged her husband. "Dad's talking to you."

Shaken from his stupor, Ashwin mumbled, "I've been thinking … You're not going to like this, Dad, but you should get a pre-nup."

"Singapore courts don't recognise pre-nups," said Sayana.

"Not true. They have enforced a few in recent years. The

problem with some pre-nups is that they short-change the wife, and that's when the Women's Charter comes in. I agree, Daddy, you should get one done," said Lavinia.

Uday shook his head. "It's such a mercenary concept—"

Ashwin shot back. "Tamara is a mercenary woman."

Uday raised his hand. "Enough! Please stop seeing Tamara like she's a gold digger who only wants me for my money. It's quite insulting. Hurtful, too. Do you really think a beautiful, highly educated woman cannot love a man like me? Sure, I'm no looker ... balding, terrible eye bags, middle-aged ..." Uday patted his belly. "A girth—yes, small for many Indian men my age, I'm told—created by alcohol and Indian food. I'm quite sure if your mother were to meet me for the first time today, she might not be quite so keen. But Tamara and I have each been given a second chance, and we're good for each other. I know I'd feel the tug if she were wrapping me around her finger." Uday wished his children would give Tamara a sporting chance.

Lavinia nodded slowly. "Fine. No pre-nup then. At least get a will—"

"I always had one. It was last updated when your mother passed away. It'll need to be updated after I get married."

"Dad, get it updated soon, and to take effect immediately upon your marriage. If, a great big if, something were to happen to you right after you got married, half of everything you have— that's right, half—goes to Tamara. We could fight it in court on the basis of her being married for less than a day, saying she should not get anything, but that's just the extreme. The reality is that without a will, she'll become the biggest shareholder of our family home."

Sayana sucked in deeply through his teeth. "Imagine that!"

9

Tamara had just returned from a fitting for her bridal dress. It was less than six weeks before their civil marriage. She placed some large paper bags on the coffee table and began opening the boxes hidden under sheaves of fine paper.

"Look, Uday! I found the perfect shoes and handbag to match my dress." She held out the bag in front of her and posed in front of Uday. "Nice?"

Uday smiled. "Everything looks nice on you, Tamara. In fact, you make everything look nicer."

"At a price! You are so generous, Uday. My friends are jealous that I'm having a Reem Acra gown. I think a few of them wore Elie Saab or Marchesa at their wedding. So common. Most of them had theirs made by tailors. Poor things couldn't afford a designer gown—"

"That sounds rather unkind. I honestly don't see why you need to spend fifteen thousand dollars on something you'll wear just once, but if it's that important to you …"

Tamara twirled, before kneeling by his feet. "Oh, Uday, it is! Besides, I'll sell it in Shanghai for about the same price, maybe even more, once I'm done. I have contacts." Tamara's eyes were twinkling. She was extremely pleased with herself. Uday could not bear to remind her that she had fallen from grace in the Shanghai social scene.

"You're obviously a lot more than just a very pretty face."

Tamara sank into the sofa and wrapped her arms around Uday. "You always know what to say, Uday." She leant back and placed her dainty feet on the coffee table. The beautiful elm wood table, made from an old Chinese door, which Tamara had bought with the money he had given her soon after she arrived. The one which Lavinia saw as a betrayal of her beloved late mother's memory. Tamara wriggled her toes, painted in a red so bright they looked like freshly pounded red chillies smeared at the tips of her feet. "Very soon I will be your wife, mistress of this luxury flat. It needs a lot of work. I will redecorate it and put it on the list of Singapore's most beautiful homes."

Uday peeled Tamara's long arms from himself and moved away from her. "No, Tamara. Please don't do anything to this place. It has been our family home for years and has grown with us. We'd like to keep it that way."

"We? You and your children? Won't I be part of your family? Won't this be my home? Won't I be part of 'we'?"

Uday stared at his clasped hands. "Let's just give the children some time to adjust to you being part of the family. It's only fair."

"How much time do you expect me to give? A year? Ten years?"

Uday inhaled deeply and took her hand. "I don't know, Tamara. But we can all make it easier on ourselves with a little understanding."

This was probably not a good time to raise a matter as delicate as a pre-nuptial agreement. Uday had agreed with Lavinia's suggestion to proceed with an updated will, which would take effect on the day of his marriage at the Marriage Registry. It was Ashwin's idea to just test Tamara's response to a pre-nuptial agreement. Uday wasn't sure he wanted to go that far. At that moment, raising the matter would be setting himself up for disappointment, and would only prove Ashwin's point, yet he was tempted to try it. Uday looked at his future wife. She was beautiful even when she was angry. He had never seen such poise in a woman.

"What? Why are you looking at me like that?"

Uday smiled and gently slid strands of her long hair from her face, tucking them behind her ears. The diamond earrings he had given her for her fortieth birthday sparkled under the halogen lights. Tamara pulled away.

"Can't a man admire the woman he is about to marry?" Uday moved closer to her. He felt his shoulders tense, as if they had a mind of their own and felt a sweat breaking at the back of his neck. How does anyone raise the subject of a document that pre-supposes a marriage is not going to last?

"Tamara, we need to talk about a pre-nuptial agreement." It was too late to revoke those words and start again with a preamble in a gentler tone.

Tamara jumped off the sofa and started screaming. "Pre-nuptial agreement? Why? You don't trust me?" She was pacing the living room, one arm on her hip. "Lavinia! I know she put you up to this. Just out of law school and thinks she's an expert on relationships! Ha!"

She was waving her finger at Uday. "She doesn't want us to get married! I've always felt that about her. She hates me. It's obvious. That's what this is all about. And don't even talk to me about a pre-nup. I won't sign it. That is the sort of thing only Western people do. Especially in Hollywood."

Tamara kicked the box, emptied of its bejewelled shoes, and stomped towards their bedroom.

"Tamara, darling. Please ..." Uday followed her, walking quickly to catch up. Grabbing her wrist, he whispered, "Tamara, please understand. It's been hard for Lavi since her mother died. They were extremely close. We all were. Please just give her some time."

Tamara glared at Uday, her nostrils flaring to the rhythm of her quick breaths. With an angry tug, she pulled away from Uday and hissed, "You've spoilt her, Uday! She's playing you against me, but you refuse to see that! No matter how much time I give, no matter how kind I am towards her, she will always hate me." She threw herself on their bed and sobbed.

Uday sat by her side and stroked her back. He should not have allowed Ashwin to talk him into testing the waters. This outcome proved nothing. Tamara was a good woman who loved him. She would make a good wife. Her parents had been respected research scientists at Stanford University, but the family had left abruptly after being accused of espionage. Tamara was fifteen and was fluent in English by then. In China, they lived comfortably under the auspices of the State.

A woman like her was not meant for a simple man. She needed someone who could keep her in the life she deserved— carefree and luxurious—while being adored. That did not make her a gold-digger. Uday was only too happy to indulge Tamara. She deserved it. He kissed her bare shoulder.

"It's all an act, Daddy. Looks like Ashwin was right." Uday turned to see Lavinia at the door. He couldn't remember the last time she had spoken to him in Hindi.

"I thought you were out."

"I was supposed to be, but changed my mind. Sorry, Daddy, but I heard everything." Lavinia stuck her tongue out like she used to when she was little and was caught telling one of her tall tales or wearing her mother's lipstick. He could not blame her for eavesdropping.

Tamara turned around. She had stopped crying, but her face was streaked with stale tears and smudged make-up. "What did you say? It's rude to speak in a foreign language in front of people who don't understand it. Your mother didn't teach you that?"

"Don't you dare speak about my mother. You're not fit to be her cleaner." Lavinia turned around, her ponytail swinging wildly, and stormed out of the room.

Sitting up, Tamara looked at Uday and said, "See? She hates me. She will do everything to keep us apart."

Uday put his arm around her, only to be rebuffed. "Time. That's all we need. Please trust me, Tamara."

"Trust you? You don't trust me! You want a pre-nup. Why? Because you think I am marrying you for your money?"

"Forget the pre-nup. We won't have one."

"Easy for you to say. Your daughter won't let you forget."

"Maybe we should give ourselves a few more months before we get married. Give the children time to get used to the idea. It's only fair. I was hasty—"

"Hasty? It's been five years!"

Uday sighed. "Tamara darling, you were married until less than a year ago. I meant that I was hasty about the marriage itself, not the intention to make you my wife."

"You want to wait? We'll wait. For as long as you want. For as long as your precious Lavinia wants. In fact, if you—no, I mean, Lavinia—wants a pre-nup, we'll have a pre-nup. Anything to make darling princess Lavinia happy."

Before he could respond, Uday heard the bathroom door slam shut.

Everything about Tamara's latest response felt odd. Her sudden acquiescence, her unusually shrill voice and the sheer mention of Lavinia's name just one time too many. Uday stood in front of the bathroom door. He needed reassurance that the stirring in his gut and the thumping in his head were due to nothing but an imagination gone just a little wild.

Uday was about to knock on the door when he heard Tamara hum a familiar tune as the shower rained on the marble floor. The tune sounded like something by Lavinia's favourite singer. He placed his ear against the door. Uday wasn't familiar with the tune but it didn't sound particularly angry.

Time was all they needed to be happy together. Forever.

10

An Evening in Mid-February

Uday looked forward to a relaxing evening with his family. Dinner together on weeknights was a ritual which had become increasingly difficult to maintain ever since Tamara moved in.

It took a lot of courage on Angela's part to tell Uday why his sons and Priyanka were suddenly working longer hours and having to eat out or in their own homes. Harder still was the confession that Lavinia's evenings doing volunteer work were largely spent at either Ashwin's or Sayana's apartment, doing data entry for an animal welfare charity. All these tactics to avoid sitting at the table with Tamara.

With Tamara in China, having been summoned by her father to visit her sick mother, Uday asked his family to gather for Sunday dinner at seven. Wati and Conchita were out on their day off, so Uday arranged for pizzas and buffalo wings to be delivered at eight.

He knocked on Lavinia's door. She did not respond. Perhaps she was in the bathroom. He opened the door, and noticing the bathroom door was ajar, spoke in a raised voice, "Lavi, your brothers and sisters are here. Join us as soon as you can, okay?" The room was still and quiet. The air-conditioner had not been on for a while. "Lavi?" Uday called her handphone. His heart beating rapidly, Uday composed himself before walking back to the living room. "Anyone heard from Lavi? She's not in her room and she's not answering her phone. I've tried twice."

Everyone checked their phones. There weren't any missed calls or messages from Lavinia.

Priyanka said, "I saw her this afternoon, when I got back from the supermarket. She was waiting for her ride to some event … I can't remember. Something to do with Monopoly."

Ashwin said, "Scrabble Sundays. She's been part of this group that meets every Sunday to play Scrabble. Friends from her first year in university."

"Yes, that's right! Lavinia was preparing for a national tournament in June. Maybe she got caught up in a game and lost track of time," said Angela. "We all know how focussed she can be."

Uday shook his head and paced the room. "She can be focussed but she was really looking forward to this evening with just us. She said she'd be back by six, as usual. She's now over an hour late and it's not like traffic is a problem on a Sunday night." Uday tried Lavinia's phone again. "Still no answer."

Ashwin offered his father a drink. "Maybe her battery's dead. I'm sure she'll turn up soon."

Uday sank slowly into an armchair, rubbing his chest. "I'm getting a bad feeling. Something has happened to her."

Priyanka, whose cousin had got killed in a drunken brawl in Delhi, said, "Don't worry, Dad. Singapore is nothing like India. Lavi will be home soon."

The family sat around and waited, each of them retreating into their own worlds, scrolling through their phones. Uday stared out of the window and wondered out loud. "Does anyone know who are her Scrabble buddies and where they meet for Scrabble Sundays?"

They looked at each other in awkward silence. Uday asked himself when he had stopped talking to Lavinia about anything and everything. He knew so much about her—her favourite things, from cakes to colours, from movies to mammals, from books to bags and even her favourite swear word. But none of these mattered when he couldn't remember her best friend's name or where she lived. He had no idea how many people were in her Scrabble Sundays group, which had been meeting now for more than four years. Maybe she had told him, but he hadn't paid attention. Or maybe she hadn't bothered to mention it because she didn't think he would be interested. The things that mattered were the things he now desperately wished he knew.

Sayana said, "I'm calling Grab. They'll be able to tell us where she was dropped off if we give them her number. We could drive there and hopefully she'll still be playing Scrabble. If not, her friends might know where she is."

After being put on hold for five minutes, he was told, "Grab does not divulge such information." Ending the call, he asked no one in particular, "Who the hell says 'divulge'? She could've said they don't provide such information. Or release, or give. Divulge? Why do Singaporeans like to use big words when there are so many normal words?"

Priyanka replied, "They think it makes them sound smart, but it really makes them sound like stupid people trying hard to sound smart. Much like most of my clients. They should stop dictating ads and leave that to us copywriters."

Uday rubbed his chin. "If she were in an accident, the police would identify her immediately from her identity card. She carries it in her wallet, right?"

"Yes, we all do. We're supposed to. So maybe she wasn't in an accident—"

Ashwin added, "Or maybe the police haven't gotten around to telling us. Maybe we should start calling the hospitals. There aren't that many."

Sayana turned to Ashwin, "Why, Ashwin? We're all trying to be positive and you must assume the worst. Why don't you just shut up until we know more?"

"I see. Sitting here scrolling our phones, checking Facebook and emails, is going to tell us what happened?"

The doorbell rang. "Pizza man. I'll get it," said Priyanka as she searched for her wallet in her handbag.

A large pepperoni pizza and a medium margherita pizza sat in open boxes next to each other on the coffee table. The buffalo wings were transferred from the box into a bowl, soggy from spilt barbecue sauce. Priyanka offered Uday some buffalo wings. "You should have something at least." Uday waved her away.

Angela tried calling Lavinia. "She's either switched off her phone or her battery's dead."

The room went quiet. Angela rested her head on Ashwin's shoulder and said she was trying not to cry.

Ashwin called the first hospital on his list. "Changi General? I'm just wondering if you have a patient named Lavinia Aurora. Yes, Lavinia. L-A-V-I-N-I-A. Last name, Aurora ... Yes! That's exactly how it's spelt. Oh, your sister's name is Aurora? Sleeping Beauty ... No, I didn't know that ... Yes, thank you, I'll hold ..." Ashwin placed a hand on the mouthpiece and asked, "Did any of you know that Aurora is Sleeping Beauty's real name?"

Priyanka took a slice of pizza. "Of course. She was also known as Briar Rose. How could you not know that?"

"I thought her name was Sleeping Beauty, and that she didn't have any other name," confessed Sayana.

Angela chuckled. "To me, she was always Shui Meiren, as she

is known in China. I only learnt about the English version when I watched a pantomime while studying here."

Ashwin took his hand off the mouthpiece. "Nothing? Alright then, thank you."

"Keep trying, Ashwin. And let's not talk about Sleeping Beauty. I'm not in the mood for frivolity." Uday knew that Lavinia still loved her Disney princesses. When channel surfing on cable television, Lavinia always stayed on a channel where a Disney movie popped up, no matter how far in it was from the beginning or how close to the end. Cinderella was her all-time favourite and Lavinia especially liked the movie with Cate Blanchett as the evil stepmother. The ballgowns are so ugly, though, she would always say. Would she have known about Sleeping Beauty's name, he wondered?

Ashwin began to call the next hospital on the list that showed up on his computer screen.

Angela asked about Charlie. She had a soft-spot for terminally ill children, having volunteered at a home for sickly, abandoned children when she was a teenager. Uday was miffed at the distraction, but perhaps that was Angela's intention. She was as compassionate and empathic as Ashwin. Uday knew they were a perfect match from the moment Ashwin brought her home, soon after meeting her at a financial conference.

"He's very ill. Last legs, I think. Tamara admitted him into hospital yesterday, before leaving for the airport. Aaron jumped at the opportunity to spend a few days in Phuket. Suits us all not to have him around."

Uday looked at his watch. Nearly nine. "She's three hours late. She hasn't called any of us. No messages from her and her phone is off. Something is wrong. We should call the police."

"They won't do anything, Dad. She's an adult so you can

only file a missing person's report after twelve hours. Let's give it another couple of hours and then we'll call the police, even if they are unlikely to do anything until later."

Uday was in his living room staring at the book on his lap. Unable to bear the oppressive air from their collective anxiety, he asked his sons and their wives to return to their own homes. Everyone promised to keep each other posted if they heard something, anything. Uday had tried watching television, surfing across every available channel. His favourite comedies failed to elicit even a chuckle.

He called Tamara. "Something bad has happened to Lavi."

"What happened?"

"I don't know. She promised to be home for dinner at six. It's now ten-thirty and still no sign of her. No calls, no messages, nothing." Tamara did not respond. "Hello? Tamara?"

"Yes, Uday. I'm here. I'm … shocked. I'm sure she's okay. Singapore is so safe."

"I have a very bad feeling, Tamara. The boys and I have decided to call the police if we don't hear from Lavi by midnight."

"The police? Isn't that too hasty? Maybe wait until the morning?"

"No. That might be too late. I should keep all the lines free, just in case. I'll speak to you tomorrow."

Uday realised he hadn't asked Tamara how she was and if her mother was feeling better. He'd call her again in the morning.

PART II

11

Ashwin was adamant about not involving the police and Uday was too distraught to fight. But he rejoined, even as he agreed to take Lavinia to their family doctor, "If the injuries are much worse than we think, we're calling the police. Damn all your plans for revenge."

"Let's take things one step at a time, Dad. If Lavi needs to be taken to hospital, the police will inevitably be involved," said Ashwin as he turned towards Sayana. "Hey, we have to go. We're taking Lavi to Dr Dubash."

Sayana walked over and took the bag from his father. "The guy I've been interrogating in Chinese, trying to find out what happened, is the good guy, Dad, and needs to get out of here. So do we."

"No, wait! He must tell us everything he knows about this before we give him a cent." Uday could not understand how a good guy found himself in such a situation, in a room with his half-dead daughter.

"He did, but now's not the time for a long chat. Let's get Lavi to the clinic quickly. Sayana looked at his sister. "You'll be okay, princess." Sayana passed the bag to the man, who limped towards Lavinia. "Stay the fuck away from her!"

The man jerked backwards and with his hands clasped in front of him, said in halting English, nodding along with every word, "Sorry, Miss. Very sorry. I no make harm for you. I think you be okay." The man bowed as he turned and shuffled out as quickly as his pummelled frame could manage.

Uday shook his head. "Alright then, call Dr Dubash. We'll take her to his clinic. He'll be able to check her and make her well."

"It's nearly 12.30am!"

"He delivered all three of you, took care of your mother. He'll expect us to call him at a time like this."

They drove to the clinic in Holland Village with Lavinia curled up in the back seat, her head on Uday's lap. The bleeding had been staunched with the help of towels from the factory. Dr Dubash was waiting for them at the parking lot in front of his clinic, with a wheelchair.

Ashwin gently lifted Lavinia onto the wheelchair, while Sayana held her limp legs and placed them on the foot rests. Standing in front of Lavinia, Uday sobbed as he watched Ashwin place her dress over her knee, her body slumped and her head dangling, as if held to her neck by a thin sliver of skin.

Shaking his head and grabbing the wheelchair handles, Dr Dubash said, "Wait at the reception. I can only offer you water from the cooler at this hour. I don't know how long this will take, but please be patient."

The three of them settled into an L-shaped sofa, underneath an air-conditioner which blasted cold air onto their faces. Ashwin found the remote control and turned it down, expecting to wait for several hours.

"Tell me all." Uday was staring at the terrazzo floor. "I want to know everything. No sugar-coating."

Sayana sat upright on the sofa and turned his face to the ceiling. Blinking a few times, he began, "His name is Ah Huat. He said his boss called him while he was in his dormitory and told him to go to the factory and wait for a man named Shaun—"

"Shaun is the monster who did this? Who the hell is he?"

"We'll soon find out. Shaun Lin or Lim, he wasn't sure. Shaun gave Ah Huat five thousand dollars—a lot of money for a butcher from Malaysia—with clear instructions to …" Sayana rubbed his hands over his face and shook his head. "You don't want to know this. Leave it to Ashwin and me to find Shaun and deal with him, Dad."

"Tell me what this monster had in mind for Lavi."

"He wanted Ah Huat to chop Lavi up into many small pieces and throw her into the two furnaces …"

Uday's eyes widened as he clutched his chest. Leaning forward, he groaned, "No. No … that's what he meant when he talked about burning Lavi? Chop her up and … no … I cannot bear this." Uday stared straight ahead, unblinking, breathing slowly and deeply. "Kill her and leave no evidence. Who? Who is the monster? Why would anyone hurt her? Do any of you have enemies who might want to hurt your sister?"

Sayana slapped his forehead. "Dad, please! Neither of us would get into situations that would result in such brutality. Nor do we know the kind of people who would retaliate like this. What about you? You're into gazillion-dollar business deals. Any egos you might have inadvertently shattered? Some people's propensity for revenge—Chinese, Thai, Indonesian, even Indian—over a perceived slight is well-documented. You interact with them more than anyone else we know. Something you know and should tell us?"

"Cut the aggression, Sayana." Uday shook his head slowly.

"I thought about that after you left. No. I can't think of anyone who would be offended by anything I might have said or done in the course of work." Uday stared at the ceiling, picturing where Lavinia was lying. "What were those furnaces for? And those massive fridges? What was that long table for?"

"It's a factory for roasting meats, mainly duck and suckling pig. They supply roasted meats to small restaurants. That whole stretch is nothing but food factories. I looked at the signs as we drove in and then back out again. There were factories for bread, cakes, tapioca crisps, dumplings and curry puffs. They're all closed on Sundays, so Shaun must have picked this date and known he wouldn't be seen."

Uday shuddered. "The table … is it for chopping up pigs and ducks?"

Sayana pursed his lips. "Probably. To prepare the meats, too, like marinating them, I think, before they are roasted."

Sayana shifted in his seat, reached into his pocket and fished out a phone. "I took this from Ah Huat. He said there are text messages with some of the bad people. We'll soon find out who Shaun is. Meanwhile, I think we need to let Shaun think Lavi is dead."

"I think I know who might have done this," said Ashwin. "I suspect Rohit—"

Uday stared at the glass shelves behind the reception counter, stacked with boxes and plastic bottles filled with medicines, and considered the possibility. Shaking his head, he spoke softly. "No. Firstly, Rohit loved Lavinia enough to want to marry her."

"I'm not sure he did. No one can really love a person and dump her just to spite her father. He was using your position and his father's relationship with you to advance his career at Fortuna Global. Everyone in Mumbai knows he's an unscrupulous thug.

Some of us believe the rumour that he beat a homeless man to death while he was in college. For sport."

"There's such a rumour? Since when? Why didn't you say something? Why did you allow your beloved sister to be involved with a criminal?"

"I'm Lavi's closest friend, Dad. You think I didn't try to talk her out of the engagement? When Rohit came here to study, I warned him that he couldn't fool me and that I was watching him. Thing is, he behaved well—mostly, not always—during those ten months. It didn't take much for Lavi to convince me that he had changed. We all wanted her to be happy. We chose to shade our eyes with rose-tinted lenses. And yes, there is such a rumour, but very few people know, and won't talk about it. There's no proof and only two witnesses, both as unreliable as Rohit."

Sayana asked, "Well, he certainly had a motive and I wouldn't put it past him. How would he have arranged it, though? With criminals who don't speak English?"

Ashwin replied, "The guy's a thug. When he wasn't seeing Lavi, he was known to hang out, and be equally comfortable, at the trendy bars and seedy karaoke joints near Chinatown. He would've made some friends where some low-lifes hang-out. For this attack, all he needed was to get *one* guy, and wire him the money. That one guy then takes care of all the details. It's not like Singapore has assassins for hire but it's also not that hard to arrange a kill. Especially if you have lots of money."

Uday looked at Ashwin with a mixture of bewilderment and daze, "How do you know all this? Singapore is so safe and clean. Wasn't it you who used to say this place is so sterile you can smell the disinfectant?"

Sayana placed his hand on his father's arm. "There's a thriving underbelly here, Dad. Just like in every big city. People blame the sudden influx of new immigrants and while they don't help, it's not like there aren't criminal elements amongst those born and raised here. Back in the old days, there were opium dens, gambling dens, and prostitution around the city. The triads controlled all these trades. It was not safe and certainly not clean. While Singapore is very safe now, I wouldn't say it's sterile."

Uday rubbed his face, as if clarity would suddenly shine through his pores. "I don't want to believe it's him but right now Rohit seems like the most likely suspect."

"Culprit," said Ashwin.

Ten minutes after wheeling Lavinia into the examination room, Dr Dubash came out to the waiting area. Uday and his sons stood up, relieved; it didn't take long, so Lavinia's condition couldn't be as bad as it appeared. It was only when Uday saw Dr Dubash standing in front of the three of them, his shoulders weighed down with the burden of having to break terrible news, that Uday stiffened and sat down.

Dr Dubash spoke slowly, "She needs to go to a hospital. And you'll need to make a police report. I've called an ambulance."

Uday shook his head. "Surely there is something you can do?"

Dr Dubash shook his head. "She was raped—"

"No! Please, no …"

"She's in a coma. The doctor at the hospital will provide more details. I am so sorry." Dr Dubash slid both hands into his pockets and looked at the floor.

Uday collapsed on to the sofa. Images of Lavinia fighting for her life while having her dignity ripped out of her flashed past him. Ashwin and Sayana sat down on each side of him, putting their arm around him. "We'll get her the best care, Dad. She is alive. Be glad for that."

Uday and his sons went outside and waited by their car. By the time the ambulance arrived, the two young men had bagged up and got rid of the bloodied towels in a bin several shophouses away.

Uday kicked a paper cup that was lying near the car. There was litter all around the half-empty carpark. After decades of fines and campaigns, parts of Singapore still reflected the habits of too many people who lacked social graces. In her teens, Lavinia had joined a few volunteers to clear litter at East Coast Park. "You're doing Lavi—and our family, for that matter—a grave injustice with your plans. Just tell the police everything!"

"I'm with Dad. You're going to screw this up, Ashwin."

"Dad, trust me please. None of you knew Lavi like I did. We were all close to her but not like I was. And you both know that. Let me handle this. Please."

The brothers called their wives, both of whom were distraught upon hearing of the attack and insisted on meeting them at the hospital. It took some effort for both Ashwin and Sayana to deflect their questions—"we don't know yet" was their stock answer—and to convince their wives to stay home for the time being.

12

The Next Morning

The emergency department was busy. It was 2am. There seemed to be a disproportionate number of migrant workers, many with bloodied arms or legs, while they waited. A number of parents were trying to comfort crying babies and feverish young children. At the triage, a sign stated that waiting time was two hours.

Ashwin spoke to a woman at the reception counter, a scrawny young woman whose temperament seemed better suited to a back-office job. Without even glancing at Ashwin, and as if speaking to her computer screen, the receptionist rattled away. "Your sister is the ambulance case from Holland Village, correct? Coma, correct? If same one, no need to wait. Your sister already with the doctor. You tell your father go through the red door—that old man is your father, correct?"

Uday glowered at the receptionist as he spoke to Ashwin. "Sort out the paper work, please. Insurance, payment, whatever. Use your credit card. We'll see you in in there." Uday dashed to the emergency room, with Sayana following just behind.

In the time it took Ashwin to wait his turn and fill in some forms to admit Lavinia as a patient, the doctor had asked Uday a few questions, called the police and ushered him and Sayana into a quiet, comfortable waiting room, where the police would soon arrive and speak to Uday and his sons.

The two police officers whispered to each other as they entered the room. After confirming that the occupants of the room were Lavinia's father and brothers, the older policeman introduced himself as Staff Sergeant Haider, before closing the door behind him and taking a seat across from Uday.

Sayana looked at the other policeman and read out his name tag. "Donald Liu." Patting his own shoulders with two fingers, referring to the epaulette, Sayana asked, "Corporal?"

The policeman nodded. "National Service." Glancing at his boss, Staff Sergeant Haider, who seemed keen to begin, he stepped back towards the door and pulled out a notepad and pen.

"Mr Aurora, please tell us exactly what happened, starting from the beginning."

Ashwin started to speak. "This has already taken a huge toll on my dad. I'll answer your questions. Is that okay?"

"Were you with your father throughout?"

"Most of the time. Lavinia was supposed to be home by six for dinner with our family."

"Where is home and where was Miss Lavinia?"

"Rose Gardens, on Grange Road. Lavinia had spent the afternoon playing Scrabble with her friends from university. They were practising for a national tournament to be held in June. She had promised to be home for dinner. She's good about keeping her commitments, especially to us … her family."

"Do you have the names of her friends, where they live?"

Sayana answered, "If we knew, we might have found her earlier, don't you think?"

Staff Sergeant Haider glared at Sayana. "No need to be rude."

Uday smacked Sayana's arm. "Exactly. Just let Ashwin answer the questions."

"We don't know much about her Scrabble group, other than that they were all at NUS together. Her closest friends are five girls from secondary school who were with her in junior college and university. She saw them on Saturday. I don't think they were in her Scrabble group."

"Do you have names or numbers?"

Ashwin pulled out his phone. "I know two of them—"

Sayana chuckled, "The ones you dated when you were in the army? I remember … sowed your wild oats by preying on our baby sister's friends."

"Shut up, Sayana." Ashwin showed Staff Sergeant Haider the phone screen before reading the contents. "Patricia Teo, 94664320. She lives in Thomson. I no longer have her address but—"

"The cops can find that in five seconds."

Uday frowned as he spoke to Sayana. "Stop being a smart aleck. It's annoying and makes you sound petty and childish."

Sayana rolled his eyes, leant back and twiddled his thumbs.

Ashwin scrolled to the next name. "Song Chun-Yi, 86639756. She used to live at Tanglin Halt, but Lavinia had mentioned the family coming into some money and moving into a terrace house along Sixth Avenue."

Uday wished he had known all this about Lavinia. He was glad that at least someone in the family knew more about her friends, her interests. If Julie were still alive, she'd know everything a mother could possibly know about her children.

"I called all the hospitals. Nothing. Called Grab Taxi, which is what we believe Lavinia took to her friend's home. They would not tell us where she went. By eight, when she was two hours late, Dad wanted to call the police, but I believe you won't do anything until six or twelve hours later. When Lavinia still had not shown up by ten, my father asked us—my brother and our wives—to go back to our homes and wait for some news. We decided we'd wait till midnight before calling the cops.

"We brothers and our wives left just after ten. About an hour later, my father received a call on the landline. The caller told my father that Lavinia was waiting to be picked up at some industrial estate in Ubi. Said he was saving her."

Staff Sergeant Haider addressed Uday. "Saving her? The caller used those words, Mr Aurora?"

Uday nodded as he stared at the floor and answered in a drained voice. "Yes. He said he was supposed to kill her, but he would save her instead. I suppose he meant he would spare her life."

"What else did he say?"

"He gave us the address, told us to hurry and hung up. We found Lavinia at the corner of Block 4008."

"Any unit number?"

Ashwin answered. "We didn't look for a unit number. The road was Ubi Avenue 2. The building was on a long street of food factories, as I gathered from the signs above the entrance to several units. I can point it out on a map to you."

Staff Sergeant Haider nodded. "Thanks. You found her on the floor? Lying down? Propped up against the wall? Was she conscious?"

"On the floor, lying down. She didn't respond when we spoke to her, so no, she was unconscious."

"Were there people around? Security guards? Anyone who might have seen someone, or a few people, driving in to drop your sister at the building?"

"There wasn't a security guard there. No guardhouse, either. The whole place was deserted. Even the car park."

The police officer pointed behind him with his pen, towards the red door. "Was Miss Lavinia in that condition when you found her? Cuts, bruises, swollen eye, slashed face, torn clothes ..."

Ashwin nodded.

Sayana rolled his eyes and whispered to Uday. "No, of course not. We did that to her."

Uday nudged him. "Stop it, Sayana."

Sayana interrupted, "My brother forgot to mention a critical detail. The caller asked for a hundred thousand dollars. At first, he asked for a million ringgit—three hundred-thousand-something at current rates—but when my father said no one could get so much at that hour, he backed down quickly. Sounds like ransom."

"A hundred thousand is still a lot of money. You gave it to him?"

Ashwin continued, "Yes. Lavinia's life for payment. Fifty thousand in cash—"

Sayana interrupted, "US dollars!"

"The other fifty thousand in jewellery, which was actually worth far more. We put everything in a bag and left it at the spot where we found Lavinia. As we drove off, we saw the bag with all that cash and jewellery was still lying there, but probably not for long."

Uday realised that no one in India would admit to having so much cash at home. It would be an invitation to get the premises raided for dirty money, for which India's elite from the business and political circles are well known.

Staff Sergeant Haider addressed Uday. "Mr Aurora, this seems like a case of kidnapping for ransom. Why didn't you call the police? Or even an ambulance, when you saw your daughter's condition?"

Uday spoke. "I called an ambulance, but my son cancelled it. We thought taking her to our family GP would do—"

"In that condition? She would have been barely alive when you found her!"

Ashwin jumped in. "I insisted on taking Lavinia to our family doctor. We had no idea how badly beaten up she was. It was dark along the corridor where we found her. As for calling the police, we know kidnapping is a capital offence, which could make this case high profile. We believed the caller when he said he was actually saving her life. Someone must have asked him to kill her, but he probably backed out when her realised he could ... he could ... sell her life. I was convinced he spared her, *he* did not kidnap her."

There was silence as Staff Sergeant Haider scanned his notes.

Ashwin added, "My father has been featured in the media in recent weeks. He won a prestigious business award last month and was in the news. Dad's picture was plastered across every newspaper in Singapore, and on the news stations, including Chinese media.

Last year, Lavinia was runner up in a Scrabble tournament sponsored by Singapore Press Holdings. The last thing we wanted was for Lavinia's plight to be made public. We were all trying to protect her." Ashwin glanced at his father, who looked at the floor as he wrung his hands. "And my dad. Our whole family, really."

Ashwin continued, "We took her straight to our family doctor, Dr Dubash. When *he* told us Lavinia needed an ambulance, we knew we would just have to deal with the publicity, if it came to that."

Staff Sergeant Haider addressed Uday. "Are you aware of anyone who might want to harm your daughter, Mr Aurora? Or maybe even you through her?"

Uday stared at the policeman and spoke in a measured tone. "I've been thinking a lot about that, trying to make sense of this evil transgression against my precious child. No! I do not have any enemies and if they wanted to cause me harm, it's not that difficult. Why would they hurt my child?"

"Because it's the most painful way to get to an enemy. Gangsters have used this tactic for years."

Uday clasped his hands and leant forward. "I can't think of anyone who would do this. Nor why."

Ashwin interrupted, "My father refuses to believe this, but I think Lavinia's ex-fiancé, a man named Rohit Gupta who lives in Mumbai, planned this. He felt shafted by my dad in the organisation his parents built from scratch, and dumped Lavinia out of spite. He had also threatened my Dad—"

Uday was livid. They had agreed not to mention Rohit. "He didn't mean it, Ashwin. It was in the heat of the moment."

Ashwin glared at Uday. "He's that kind of guy, Dad." Turning to Staff Sergeant Haider, Ashwin said, "I'm sure Rohit has something to do with it. Here's his mobile number, and his home number, too."

"We'll need Miss Lavina's phone, please, assuming she still has it. We also need to go through her things, diaries and any journals. The culprit is still at large, so we need to act quickly. We don't know if he or she meant to kill Miss Lavinia or hurt her, maybe to send a message. Mind if we go over to your home now to retrieve these?"

Uday gave Staff Sergeant Haider his address and assured him that either Wati or Conchita would let them in. "We ourselves would like to stay here until the doctor gives us an update on Lavinia's condition."

The doctor met Uday and his sons in the waiting room. "Lavinia has severe brain injury. She may have fallen or been pushed backwards and hit her head against a hard surface. Lavinia was raped, possibly by two, perhaps three men—"

Uday sobbed as he leant towards Sayana.

"I'm very, very sorry, Mr Aurora. She also has multiple fractures on her hands, which could suggest she was fending off blows. At this point, there is no telling how long she'll be in a coma."

"But she will recover, yes? With the best medical care, she will regain consciousness? Won't she?"

The doctor took a deep breath, looked at the folder on his lap and pursed his lips before he replied, "Mr Aurora, with severe brain injury, there is no way of telling how well the patient will recover. I can give you statistics, but they won't mean a thing at this point. We'll need to monitor Lavinia for the next two weeks. She will be in the ICU and will receive the best care." The doctor looked at his watch. "It's nearly 4am, Mr Aurora. You and your sons should go home. Get some rest. You can spend some time with Lavinia before you go. Try and have a family member visit her every day."

It was Ashwin's turn to drive. A phone rang while they were on their way home. It was not a ringtone they recognised.

Uday yelled, "It's that fellow's phone! It's probably Shaun, or whatever his name is, wanting an update! Who has the phone?"

Sayana reached into his pocket, switched off the radio and answered the phone in Chinese. He sounded rough, unlike the refined way he spoke when ordering a meal in a restaurant.

"Hello?" The voice on the other end echoed in the car. Sayana spoke mainly in monosyllables, with the exception of two sentences. At one point, Sayana pulled the phone away from his ear, so far and so quickly that it hit the window. He gestured to Ashwin to pull over to the side. Ashwin turned into a quiet street just off Zion Road.

The call ended within two minutes. Sayana turned to face Uday. "I'm quite sure that was Shaun. Sounded like a woman. Definitely not a man."

"A woman? I heard all that screaming. Maybe it was a man who sounded like a woman?"

Sayana shook his head. "It was a woman, Dad. She assumed I was Ah Huat and asked what happened to the photos of Lavinia's pieces. I said I had no time. She swore, using typical Chinese phrases—all extremely vulgar—and said she will never order roast meats from my uncle again. She asked how long before the parts turned to ash. I said at least another four hours, and even then there'd still be a few bones."

Uday covered his ears. "This is too morbid!"

"She told me to meet her at the factory at ten in the morning. She said she wanted the ashes because … forget it, not important."

"Because what? Tell us, Sayana!" demanded Uday.

"Because she wanted the pleasure of flushing them down the loo."

"That's one sick bastard," said Ashwin.

Sayana replied, "I'm going to turn up at the factory before ten and try to get more information."

Uday did not like the idea of his son confronting a violent thug all alone. "I'm not sure you should go. I mean, what will you do when, or if, you see Shaun? How would you know it's him or her? He might send a friend."

"It's the only way I can get to know who Shaun is. I'll watch from the car and take pictures. I'll trail her, or whoever turns up for the ashes. I'll have to be there to find out."

Uday looked at his watch. "That's six hours from now. I don't think any of us will be at work tomorrow but Sayana, you need to go to sleep right away. Both of you, tell your wives as little as possible, and swear them to secrecy. I'll do the same with Tamara."

13

Later That Morning

Uday was on tenterhooks as he waited for a report from Sayana, who was waiting for Shaun near the factory, with Ah Huat's phone fully charged and in his pocket. After the first phone call from his father, Sayana was diligent about providing updates every ten minutes, including evocative details which made Uday feel as if he was actually there, trailing his beloved daughter's attacker.

A1 Roasted Meats was closed. Sayana put his ear against the aluminium shutters. All he heard were ambient sounds from the industrial refrigerators, other shops and the main road. He took a step back and read the signs and posters, hoping to find information about opening hours.

"Today close! Sunday Monday always close," said a young woman stacking plastic crates filled with dumplings waiting to be steamed, at the entrance to the factory next door.

Sayana spoke in Chinese. "Do you know the people who work here? I need to order three suckling pigs for a friend's wedding. Last-minute, and I heard this was the best."

The woman giggled. "Wah, *ang mo* speak Chinese so good."

Sayana laughed. He was used to being referred to by the word commonly used to describe white people. He replied in Chinese,

"No, no, no ... I'm not *ang mo*. Indian father, half-English mother. Studied Chinese in school. Do you know how I can contact them? I can't find the number anywhere."

The woman smiled and responded in English. "Your Chinese very good. Sorry, I don't know people work here." She peered into her shop and tried to find her boss. "You wait. I ask my boss." The woman returned and said in a sheepish voice, "Boss tell me must mind my own business. Sorry, cannot help you."

Sayana thanked her and walked to the end of the row of shop-factories. He spotted his favourite cake in a glass cake display at the corner cake shop. He laughed at the name, Sweet Cherry Cakery. Was that even a word? Sayana wondered what Lavinia would think and if she would dare use it in Scrabble. He bought a slice of Pandan Chiffon and bit slowly into the narrow edge of the fluffy green cake. This was the best breakfast he'd had in weeks.

Ah Huat's phone buzzed. It wasn't Shaun's number. Sayana looked to his right. The space outside A1 Roasted Meats was empty. There were a few people along the corridor, all of whom seemed to be preoccupied with loading or unloading crates or boxes of food.

Sayana declined the call and walked towards the carpark behind the building. Two people stood outside the back door where, barely ten hours earlier, Sayana had waited to be let in with his brother and father. One of them stood behind a rubbish bin. Sayana could see only the top half of him. He stood out for wearing a hoodie in this unbearable heat. The glare from the blazing sun hitting the white concrete was blinding. Nibbling on his cake while keeping a surreptitious eye on the men who seemed deep in conversation, Sayana walked towards his car. Soon after he got in, the phone buzzed again. Sayana had parked his car so it faced the back of the building. He could see them clearly, but it was unlikely they could see him, due to the glare on the windscreen. He put on his sunglasses and took the call.

"Where are you? We are waiting outside. Back door."

Sayana sounded breathless. "I'm running from the bus stop. You said ten. It's only nine forty-five! I'll be there soon." Sayana ended the call and stared at the two young men waiting for Ah Huat.

Of the two people, the one on the phone sounded like the one who had called early that morning. The one named Shaun, who Sayana had thought was a girl. She had heavy features and short, spiked hair which accentuated her square face, but went well with her small frame. Both her arms were tattooed in their entirety. She wore black trousers rolled up at the ankles and cinched at her midriff, possibly unable to find anything suitable for her short legs and small waist. Her baggy tee-shirt was tucked into her trousers and her sleeves were rolled up to her shoulders. She had the gait of a schoolyard bully. Sayana stared at her. Shaun didn't look like a girl. Her chest was flat. Perhaps his father was right, and Shaun was a man who sounded like a woman and, by the looks of it, was built like a boy. For now, he agreed with Uday and assumed Shaun was a man. The other person was wearing the hoodie and was squatting as he smoked a cigarette. Moments later, the smoker stood up, removed his hoodie and took a water bottle from Shaun's backpack.

"Wow, oh wow! I can't believe this!" Sayana laughed when he realised he was talking to himself. When he called next, Uday had to remind him that he was supposed to be taking photos, not just engaging in surveillance. Sayana promised he would, but was unable to get face shots, as Shaun kept facing the door to the factory, his back towards him.

While Sayana wasn't sure of Shaun's gender, it was obvious by now that Shaun's friend was a young girl, probably no more than eighteen. She was slightly taller than Shaun and had long hair dyed a shade of blonde so wrong it looked like freshly beaten egg yolks. She wore denim shorts which were frayed at the edges and short enough to get her flogged in some countries. Her legs were dotted with scars, probably from mosquito bites. She was pretty in an impish way and was probably Shaun's girlfriend. He took photographs of both of them.

Shaun looked like he was getting impatient, pacing the back of the building and kicking bits of litter along the way. Sayana was suffocating in the sweltering car but could neither turn on the engine nor wind the windows down.

The phone rang again.

Shaun raised the mouthpiece to his lips and screamed into it. "Hurry up or you'll soon be joining the girl!"

Sayana smiled. "Really? And who will kill me? You? And chop me up? You are all talk, no action. You stupid, cowardly fuck!" Sayana had to suppress the urge to laugh when he saw Shaun staring ahead, to Sayana's left, mouth gaping, while his girlfriend appeared to ask what was going on. Sayana continued, "You know what? You go get the ashes yourself. Lots of bones, too. You didn't pay me enough to do such dirty work. I'm going back home! You don't know me, you won't know where to find me. I'll tell my boss all about you. He's my uncle, okay? Imagine if he knew you lied to him, you used him for such evil. He thought you needed the fridge because yours had broken down late last night and you needed to keep your seafood chilled. I'll tell him you needed the furnaces instead, to burn a young woman! I'll say you killed her. So, don't think you're some big shot who can bully me." Sayana hung up, pleased at his ability to speak the unrefined form of Chinese he had picked up in the army.

Watching Shaun squat and bury his head in his hands made him value Ah Huat's information more than either of them had thought possible.

Shaun spoke to his girlfriend, who offered him a cigarette. He rubbed his face and squeezed his girlfriend's hand before calling again. His voice was soft this time. "I need the ashes. Please. I'm sorry. It's hot and I'm under pressure."

"Pressure? What pressure? You mean you are a runner for someone? Tell me who and I'll help you clear out the furnace."

"You're just a butcher. Why are you asking so many questions? It's none of your business."

"You want the ashes or not?"

"I can't tell you anything. You're being too clever for your own good. Just be careful. Five thousand is a lot of money. I'll find a way to—"

Sayana hung up and waited. Perhaps they would head home, or to work.

Shaun looked as if he was searching for something on his phone. Sayana took some pictures while he had the chance. Minutes later, Sayana saw the girlfriend raise her arm, as if to hail a taxi. As soon as the red Honda Vezel pulled up in front of them, Sayana switched on the ignition, turned the air-conditioning up full blast and followed the Honda.

Uday tried to talk Sayana out of this part of the surveillance, fearing he might get too close and be attacked or killed by Shaun. Sayana assured Uday he would be fine. Shaun and his girlfriend looked too petite to be dangerous. Besides, even if there was a knife or any weapon in the girlfriend's backpack, Sayana, a black-belt in Aikido, would be able to take her down before she could get to the bag.

It was half an hour before the car entered a housing estate and dropped them off at Block 408, Clementi Avenue 6. As the two dawdled towards the lift, Sayana parked his car and dashed in to the lift as well. He ushered them in first—they didn't even thank him or acknowledge his politeness, rude guys.

Seeing that they had pressed 8 on the lift number panel, Sayana pressed 7.

Shaun whispered in Chinese to his girlfriend, "The *ang mo* looks familiar. We've seen him somewhere, haven't we?"

Sayana stiffened. He pretended to be reading messages on his phone. His cover was blown. He had been too confident, and Shaun was one step ahead of him.

The girlfriend turned around and glanced at Sayana. She replied "Yes, on television. He's that actor who plays a doctor on a Channel 5 serial. He's quite famous. Surprised to see him around here."

"No. I don't think it's because he's an actor. I've seen him before."

Sayana was relieved when the lift stopped on the seventh floor. He wished them a good day and waited at the landing for the lift to open on the next floor up. As they alighted, he tip-toed up the stairs, following their voices. They were now walking down the corridor. From behind the wall of the lift lobby, Sayana saw Shaun's girlfriend opening the door as Shaun followed behind. The door banged shut. Sayana walked towards the flat, the third unit from the corner. #08-1034.

Sayana had an address, a phone number, a sort of confession and possibly the name of a person of unconfirmed gender. He now had to figure out what to do with the information. Although he was exhausted and in need of some sleep, he felt energised about getting closer to the person who tried to kill Lavinia.

Uday was proud of his self-righteous son who, for once, willingly agreed to participate in a clandestine operation in support of his family's search for justice.

Uday agreed with Sayana that it was highly unlikely Rohit—still their main suspect—who did not understand a word of Chinese, would be directly in touch with Shaun, who probably spoke very little English. Sayana was convinced Shaun was merely carrying out instructions, and was determined to find out who Rohit had hired to kill Lavinia.

14

That Afternoon

They're all here. The only men in Lavinia's life. The only men in mine. Uday is beside himself. He stares at Lavinia's bandaged head, her hair shaved for the emergency surgery early that morning. Pus oozes from one side of the face. He stretches out his arm to stroke her face and pulls back, covers his face and sobs.

Ashwin and Sayana are more composed as they stand beside him and pat his shoulders. I am in so much pain seeing him like this. I run my hands through his hair. He freezes and looks at his sons. He says nothing and slides both his hands down the sides of his head, as if convincing himself he had done the same a moment ago. I stop and take my seat on the other side of the bed, by Lavinia's feet. Like me, she would be pleased to see her brothers come together in peace, both putting their intense grief ahead of their petty differences.

Angela had dropped by in the late morning. She brought white tulips with fuchsia tips, which looked like someone painstakingly painted with light brushstrokes near the tip of every petal. They really brighten up the room. It's quite a nice room, decorated and furnished like a three-star hotel in England. The machines make the room less congenial than the other wards but there's a sofa—in dark green synthetic leather with hard cushions—for a family member to sleep on. It's ugly, like those boxy, functional designs from the seventies, but it's comfortable. There's also an armchair. There's a small desk with a flimsy wooden chair, which Uday has placed by Lavinia's bed, so he can sit as he speaks to her. Unlike the other wards, the ICU rooms do not have television.

As public hospitals go, this is excellent. Uday had mentioned earlier that he'd like to move Lavinia to a private hospital but thankfully Sayana knocked some sense into him, telling him that Singapore's government hospitals are said to have better facilities and the best doctors.

Uday stops sobbing and is breathing slowly. "Please get well, Lavi. For all of us. Your brothers are here with me. Pri will drop by this evening, after work." His voice is soft.

As soon as Uday seems a bit less distraught, Sayana tells him what he's found out about Shaun. Uday stares at the photos and complains he can barely see Shaun's face, but he can tell Shaun looks like a boy. If I had not insisted on the boys studying Chinese and in one of Singapore's top schools, too, I doubt Sayana would've have made this much progress in his investigations. Ashwin had struggled and switched to Hindi within a year, but Sayana persevered and aced the subject. Brownie points for me, thank you.

Uday stops listening to Sayana and turns to Lavinia, lowering his voice. "We're going to find out who did this to you. Your brothers are working on it. Sayana found the boy who took you to the factory. Imagine that, a boy! We will deal with him ourselves. The police don't have enough information to be ahead of us. We even gave them a different block number, the one *next* to where we actually found you. Oh, Lavi, my beloved Lavi … No matter how good the police are, no matter how fair the judge might be, the law will never provide enough justice for what they did to you."

Uday is right. Lavinia might one day be well enough to go home but it's hard to say how well she'll recover. Severe brain injury. The doctor said that a few times, the last being this morning when he brought in a team of medical students. I resented them all talking over her like she was some specimen. But I had to accept that this was a teaching hospital and the intrusion was a small price to pay to be treated by the country's best doctors.

Sayana stares at his sister as he speaks: "I don't know how Shaun could have inflicted so much damage. He looks like a teenage boy and his girlfriend can't be more than eighteen. Shaun had tattoos all over and walked like a gangster so maybe he is both violent and strong. I just wonder where Rohit found him."

Rohit? How did Rohit become part of this? He savaged Lavinia's heart at the start of the year. He would not then go on to inflict such barbarity on her body and her soul. I do not like him, but I don't believe he has anything to do with this.

Shaun is not a boy. He is a she. I know this because when I tried to stop her from hitting Lavinia, I accidentally rubbed against her breasts. It felt like she had bound them tightly. I'm sure Sayana will find out Shaun's real gender soon.

Rohit could never have arranged this. I was with Lavinia when she got into one of those shared private hire taxis. It was around 5pm, and raining heavily. The driver told her she would be the last one to be dropped off, after the other two men. He took them to an industrial park near Macpherson. The two got off, but the driver did not leave. He switched off his engine. I realised that something was wrong. Then the door on the left, on Lavinia's side, opened. She screamed for barely a few seconds when one of the men stuffed a cloth in her mouth and taped over it. She reached for her phone, but the other man grabbed her handbag. I held her tightly, so he wouldn't be able to pull her out of the car. I didn't know how to get the driver to zoom off with us. The next moment, the driver got into the back seat from the right and pushed us out. He was part of the plan! I tried but could not fight him.

The driver left whilst the two men took Lavinia by her arms, one on each side, and directed her to a cargo lift which took them to the third floor, where she was then forced into a room which might have until recently been an office. There were grey metal partitions with glass which started halfway and went up to the ceiling. The floor was cement, which looked roughly applied and had strips of glue all over, presumably residual glue from carpet or linoleum flooring which had been ripped out.

Poor Lavinia—I saw the terror in her eyes and I heard her scream even though there wasn't a sound from her taped mouth. "Mama, come! Mama!" I told her I was there. She knew when I put my hands around her face and kissed her. The two men made a few calls. They spoke in Chinese. They bound Lavinia's hands and feet and told her to sit on the floor and wait. They left, locking the door behind them.

Lavinia dragged herself close to her handbag. I pushed her as much as I could. Together, we got the phone out but neither of us could make a call. By the time Lavinia managed to wriggle her hands and feet out of those ropes, her phone battery was dead. We tried to get out of the office, but the door was double locked and there was nothing with which to break it. Lavinia banged on the door and the walls. But it was Sunday and all the offices were closed.

It was nine o'clock before those two showed up—Shaun and her sidekick, the Chinese girl with blonde hair. The two men were now accompanied by a third fellow. When Shaun saw that Lavinia was neither tied nor gagged, she went ballistic and started kicking the two men. For a puny thing, she packed quite a punch. Lavinia turned to me and begged me not to let any of the bad people in the room touch her. I tried. Oh, how I tried! As hard as any mother, who would give her life for her child's.

Then it began, first with kicking and beating. Shaun sat on top of her and whipped out a pen knife. *No! No, don't do that!* I screamed. With one quick flick of her wrist, Shaun slashed the right side of Lavinia's face, from just below her cheekbone to her chin. Lavinia's mouth was taped but I could hear her piercing shriek, her pain shattering my heart. I swooshed around Shaun just enough to distract her before she tried to inflict the same, deep gash on the left side of Lavinia's face. Except, even then, I was a little too late. Shaun still managed to make a small, superficial cut on Lavinia's other cheek.

There were five of them; I could not shield my baby. The two women watched as two men raped Lavinia and the third tried but failed. He couldn't. You know what I mean. He was probably too scared, because he ran away leaving the rest behind. Lavinia was in a daze when she tried to stand up after the third fellow ran away. I stood behind Lavinia to support her. Shaun pushed her with both her hands. Lavinia stumbled but quickly regained her balance. I got in front of Lavinia so Shaun wouldn't be able to push her again, but I was too late. Shaun pushed her so hard this time that she fell and hit her head against the cement floor. Lavinia went still. Shaun made a few calls.

Two men carried Lavinia and dumped her in the back of a pick-up truck. One of the rapists drove to that food factory. Poor girl, all bruised and battered, lying unconscious in the back of a filthy, blue pick-up. I got in and lay next to Lavinia with my arms across her chest as I sang her a song. *Bridge Over*

Troubled Water. When Lavinia was born a month premature, she was extremely fragile and needed constant care and attention for the first few weeks. Rather than a common lullaby, I wanted something which would express my commitment to her forever. Uday liked the song so much, he made it our family anthem.

Lavinia was bleeding from the back of her head. I placed my hand at the source of all that blood but could not stem the flow. I was so scared she would die. I spoke to her, sang to her. I even prayed with her, something I hadn't done in years. I had no idea where we were going. We seemed to have been driving, mostly on highways, for a long time, at least an hour. I didn't recognise the roads or the buildings. Uday and I used to joke about how if you drove for an hour in Singapore, you would land in the sea. Singapore's not that tiny, though, is it? Not with the network of highways that seem to go on forever.

When we got to that factory, the whole place was deserted. Shaun called the man who was waiting inside and demanded he open the door quickly. The chubby fellow scowled as he let them in. I didn't understand what they were saying but he kept pointing to his watch, so I think he was called specifically to be at the factory to wait for Shaun. The rapist sat in the car. Shaun's girlfriend lit a cigarette while the man in the factory—his name was Ah Huat—and the other rapist lifted Lavinia out of the back of the pick-up truck. Ah Huat was gentle with her but he ranted all the way. After seeing that Lavinia was lying unconscious on the table, Shaun said something and took out a lot of money. I don't know how much, but they were all fifty-dollar notes. Quite a few stacks. I'd guess at least five thousand dollars. Ah Huat waved them away, shaking his head and waving his hands in front of him. He didn't want to take the money, but it also sounded like he didn't want to do what Shaun asked him. Shaun probably threatened Ah Huat and offered him more money. Looked like a few thousand dollars. I realised then that she was telling Ah Huat to kill her.

I watched as Shaun walked to the two furnaces and shovelled in a bagful of charcoal in each. They were huge cylinders with a pitched roof on top, like a small grain tower with a chimney. The vents on the roof were attached to thick corrugated pipes which led outside. Shaun threw in some fire starters and set the furnace alight. He was going to burn Lavinia alive! I tried to extinguish the flames, but I just couldn't. I tried to lock the furnace so no one could open it, but here too, I failed.

Shaun then walked towards Ah Huat, yelling. Sounded like he was asking for something. Ah Huat went towards a cupboard and removed two cleavers. Big, sharp things. I was petrified. Was he going to chop her into pieces before burning her? *She's not dead,* I shrieked, and there must have been a sound because the two of them stared at each other and asked where that noise came from. I kept shrieking and pushed myself against Shaun. I used all the force I never even knew I had. I could feel Shaun's resistance. She was trembling, her eyes searching for whatever it was that was forcing her back. She could not see my rage, my fear, but I made sure she felt both.

Shaun stammered as she spoke to Ah Huat, who remained silent and stared at Lavinia. I saw so much sadness in Ah Huat's eyes that I felt sure he would not hurt her. I turned around, just in time to see Shaun sprinting towards the back door. Within minutes, she came back inside and chucked Lavinia's handbag across the floor, without saying a word. I suppose she wanted that burnt along with her cut-up pieces.

I sat up, next to Lavinia's inert body. Ah Huat kept staring at her. He looked at the stash of fifty-dollar notes lying at the end of the cold, steel table. He shook his head. He put his hands around her neck. I must have been mistaken! Those sad eyes must have meant something else. Such big hands on the slender neck of an unconscious young woman would mean a quick death, but I wasn't about to let Lavinia die. Not at the hands of this low-life butcher.

I swirled around him, rapidly, left to right and right to left. He released his grip and stumbled backwards. He looked dizzy. He breathed in deeply as he looked around. He picked up the cleaver. I whirled and twirled like a dervish dancing in a trance, churning the air around him. He dropped the cleaver, jumped back and looked around again. He spoke in English, "Who you? Who?" He felt someone was watching him and wasn't about to let him chop up the beautiful young woman.

His eyes scanned every square inch of the factory, stopping when he saw the bag. He walked towards it and searched the contents. He looked inside her wallet, closed it and shoved it into his back pocket. He sat on the floor, leaning against the fridge, and scrolled through Lavinia's phone. I stood next to him. He must have felt something because he got up and waved his arms, as if pushing me away.

He stared at the money in front of him. He went back to scrolling on Lavinia's phone. He found "Home" and called Uday, and then hung up before it rang. He hesitated for a good ten minutes, sobbing in between. He poured water into the furnace and covered the smouldering charcoal with a metal dome.

Sayana was wrong—Ah Huat was not the good guy. There wasn't one in that horror show. Ah Huat would have killed her and chopped her up if I had not stopped him. Fear, not goodness, kept him away from her. Greed led him to ransom what was left of her young, precious life.

I saw what happened. I want to see those wretched creatures dead. Everyone involved in Lavinia being in this condition must pay for this. I know Uday and the boys are angry enough to want the same. Ashwin is rogue enough to make it happen and Sayana is clever enough to ensure no one gets caught.

15

A Few Hours Later

Uday checked his phone when he returned from the hospital. In his haste, he had left it charging by his bedside, after several long calls to his office in Singapore and Mumbai. Six missed calls and twelve messages from Tamara.

Tamara answered even before the phone could start ringing. "Uday! Where have you been?"

Uday let out a huge sigh. "I've just experienced the worst two days of my life. Lavi is in hospital. A terrible thing happened last night. I meant to call this morning, but things happened so quickly, and next, I collapsed from exhaustion. When I woke up, I rushed to the hospital, leaving my phone at home. I'm so sorry for not calling sooner."

"Oh no! What happened, Uday? Is she going to be alright?"

"She was attacked last night. She's in a coma. No idea how long it'll be before she recovers."

"Attacked? By whom?"

Uday was about to mention Shaun when he remembered his pact with the boys about saying as little as possible to their wives. "No idea. The boys and I are looking into it."

"Did you call the police?"

"No. The hospital did that. They are supposed to if they

suspect a patient was the victim of a crime."

"What did you tell them?"

"Whatever we knew, which was nothing much. The boys and I are working on it."

"Working on what? Are you doing the job of the police?" Tamara's tone was antagonistic. She was probably worried about him getting into trouble, especially as he could be dealing with hardened criminals.

"No, Tamara. We are just trying to find out who did this to Lavi. The police have nothing to go with right now. We'll be okay, don't worry. How are you? How is your mother?"

"I'm alright. Worried about you, that's all. My mother is still very sick, but she won't get better with me staying here longer. Also, I miss Charlie. Maybe I should get on the next flight."

Uday realised Lavinia would hate the thought of Tamara visiting her in hospital. "We've got everything under control. There's always someone by Lavinia's side during visiting hours. Angela insists on sleeping at the hospital tonight. She's safe. Stay with your mother as long as you need to."

"Let's not pretend, Uday. Lavinia hates me. I'm flying back for *you*. This must be so hard. I want to be by your side."

Uday was struck by Tamara's voice. It was as icy as the winter air gets in Shanghai. He wasn't sure her presence would be a source of comfort. "She doesn't hate you. With so much going on, and with new projects coming up, I'm going to be too distracted over the next few days to focus on anything or anyone except Lavinia."

"Lavinia this, Lavinia that … Sorry about what happened. Let me know if you want me back earlier. If not, I'll see you in a week."

Uday's head throbbed. "Alright, then. I'll call you tomorrow evening." Uday crawled under his sheets, hoping to get some sleep before going over to Sayana's for dinner, and, more importantly, a discussion, in complete privacy.

There was a knock on the door. Uday was not quite asleep, his mind still racing.

"It's us, Dad," said Ashwin. "I dug up some info. Sayana's with me."

"Come in." Uday drew the curtain aside and sat up in his bed.

Ashwin whizzed past Sayana and ran towards Uday, clutching his laptop. "I think I've made a breakthrough, Dad! With the information Sayana gave us this afternoon, I Googled Shaun Lin. Listen to this …" Ashwin switched on the television screen and plugged the cable into his laptop. His hands danced across the keyboard as page after page was pulled up.

"What's all this? They look like random websites and conversations on forum pages," said Sayana as he noticed Uday staring at the screen, frowning and squinting, trying to read some of the text which disappeared as Ashwin pulled up a new page.

"Here! Found it." Ashwin stood behind the television screen and pointed to a specific line. "Says here, 'Got chef name Shaun Lin work at Sin Hoe Hin. Use him two time oredi for private party. His food damn good leh.'"

Sayana cringed. "Atrocious English! I don't care what they say, it's not Singlish. Just bad English, plain and simple. Why can't Singaporeans get their grammar basics right and spell words properly rather than how they pronounce it? Oredi for already? Seriously? Sheesh!"

Ashwin smirked as he replied, "I know! Must be hard for you, the pedantic English teacher at an elite school."

"Focus! Let's get back to this, please," said Uday.

"I Googled the restaurant—Sin Hoe Hin. It looks like it's

very popular. Famous for … guess what? Suckling pig! And it's at Clementi Street 10, which is very close to where Shaun lives. Apparently, on Mondays, when the restaurant is closed, Shaun freelances as a private chef. He charges three hundred an evening for dinner. That's just to cook the meal. Taxi fares and all ingredients have to be paid for by the host. I scrolled down and went through three pages before someone had posted a number. It's the one you have on Ah Huat's phone. Voila! This chef, Shaun, is Lavi's attacker!"

"So? How is it a breakthrough, Ashwin? I'm the one who got his address. Photos, too! How does your information help us any more than what we had before you decided to play P.I.?"

"Okay, Sayana, you're the clever one. Everyone knows that. So, tell me, what exactly were you going to do with your information?"

"How do you know it's the same Shaun Lin? There might be a few of them around. We don't know for sure our guy, or girl, is a chef. The only connection you have now is the suckling pig. You get the wrong person and you'll ruin us all!"

"I'm hundred percent sure he's the one. I checked Google images and … look!" Ashwin pulled up a page with several images of a chef who looked like the boy-girl Sayana had photographed that morning. "That's the same Shaun! Now we know more about him, it might be easier to get him. For someone so smart, Sayana, you should have thought about this earlier."

"Please. My pictures aren't clear enough for you to make a definitive identification."

"Looks clear enough to me, especially when comparing your photos to the one I Googled. Can we just assume this is the same Shaun Lin? Only thing now is to establish if Shaun is a man or a woman."

"I'm not the one who spends my time on rubbish sites like you do. Which site is this? eateatdrinkdrink.com? Even the name is so stupid! Must reflect the quality of the conversations there. No better than what's on the screen."

"There's useful information on good places to eat, especially for hawker food. These people are really passionate about food. You're just a snob, Sayana! Your loss."

Uday stretched out his arms and waved them up and down, as if to quieten young children. "Boys, please. Stop arguing. We have a name and address. We have some photos. But who is he? Or she? Was it really Rohit who hired this creature to kill Lavi? If not, then who did? So many questions still to be answered."

Ashwin sat next to his father. "I don't know, Dad. I know you don't believe Rohit was involved, but I do. I think as a start, I'll call Shaun and book a private event with him—"

"I don't want to wait till next Monday! Let's try and get him earlier. Offer him more. How much do you think he makes a month? Two thousand dollars?"

"Yes, around that, from what I gathered on this forum. Someone said that as a private chef who has a gig every week, Shaun Lin can make more than half his salary in four days. We should offer him double."

Sayana stood in front of Uday and Ashwin. He had his thumbs looped through his belt hoops. "Then what? He comes over and what do we do with him?"

"We force all the information out of him."

Sayana laughed. "Oh, I see. Like he's going to volunteer everything like people usually do, especially when they've committed a crime."

"Of course not. We'll threaten him with torture first, and then resort to actual torture if we must. We can have him over at my flat. I'll ask Angela to come over here while we sort some things out. She'll probably work late all this week anyway."

"At what point does torture turn to murder? There are criminals who would much rather die than be a rat."

Uday spoke. "It's good that we have identified Lavi's attacker. It's good that we know where to find him. But we still need to find out who was behind this."

He yawned. "I need a shower to wake up. Sayana, you really need to get some sleep as well. So do all of us. Let's skip dinner at Sayana's and have an early night. I'll be in the office tomorrow morning. Ashwin, I'll see you at the hospital at 2pm. Let's think about this again tomorrow and discuss our options. For now, Lavi is safe. Shaun thinks she's gone."

"Shall we meet here tomorrow evening?"

Uday shook his head. "I'd rather we meet at Sayana's. With Pri working late, it'll be just us. I want Shaun to pay for what he did, but I don't know where to begin. We need to think this through carefully. In private."

Sayana shrugged. "Sure. I'll be home by six. I'd apply for emergency leave, but with mid-term exams coming up next month, I owe it to my students to be full-on at school."

"I understand. Ashwin managed to get leave all this week, so that'll help a lot. I'll work from home, but I have to go in tomorrow morning for an hour or so."

Sayana glanced at the clock on Uday's bedside table. "Don't you have that office dinner, Dad? Tonight at seven, right?"

Uday bounced out of his bed. "Oh damn, you're right! I'll have to cancel it. No … I can't. I invited some bigwigs from Shanghai Building Company. They extended their stay just for this celebration. They hinted at fish head curry at Jupiter."

"What's with the Chinese and fish head curry? I just don't get it."

"Nor do I, but I must get ready. I'm already late. I'll go for an hour. Please, if you can, pop in to see Lavi before dinner."

16

That Night

Uday Aurora stepped outside the Jupiter Banana Leaf restaurant for a cigarette. It was his first cigarette since he quit smoking over a year ago. What he really needed was a Scotch. But not here. Not in this ageing restaurant with plastic table covers and pale green melamine plates shaped like mutated banana leaves and certainly not with his employees.

Uday could never understand the appeal of the restaurant's specialty and one of Singapore's favourite dishes—a fish's head swimming in a tamarind gravy, eyes bulging and mouth slightly open, exposing opaque white teeth which looked like the tiny thorns on the stem of a rose in full bloom. Try it, Mr Aurora! The cheeks are plump with succulent flesh, they said. And the curry, so tangy, so addictive. No thank you, he said. I'll just order myself a vegetarian biryani.

Still struggling to cope with last night's tragedy, Uday had tried to avoid this evening's event, but found it impossible to extricate himself without giving a good reason. This was a small price to pay for clients from Guangzhou who had been nothing but honourable since he was introduced to them years ago. He had promised to join them for an hour, before visiting someone. He glanced at his watch. He could leave soon; a few would make the obligatory fuss, but not enough to compel him to stay.

It was nearly 9pm. A gentle breeze cutting through the warm air wafted the faint smell of stale urine from a back alley nearby. Race Course Road was bustling with migrant workers from India and Bangladesh, shopping for groceries, just milling about chatting with each other, or on the phone, presumably with their families back home. Uday felt sorry for them. Having lived in Singapore for nearly fifteen years, he had heard enough horror stories to know that a typical migrant worker's life was a tale of woe. For a number of men squatting or sitting along the pavement across the street, the unflattering street lights served to deepen the lines of misery on their weather-beaten faces.

Up until yesterday, Uday did not have it in him to hurt anyone. He had turned vegetarian when he was twelve, after going to the meat market near an abattoir in Mumbai with his family's cook and witnessing a young goat being slaughtered there. He had run towards the butcher and hit him, wailing and begging him to release the goat, it's ear-splitting bleat sounding like a wailing baby desperate for his feed. Young Uday had been inconsolable for days, before proclaiming his decision to never eat meat again. The thought and sight of blood and violence still sickened him.

Several people were leaving the restaurant. A blast of air-conditioning hit him every time someone opened the door. Despite the artificially cool air around him, Uday felt the heat rising within him. He breathed more rapidly. Watching the migrant workers—some boisterous, most subdued, all probably struggling to make ends meet—Uday made up his mind.

He took a long, deep draw on his cigarette and called his chauffeur to pick him up.

In the living room of his spacious apartment on the twentieth floor, Uday sipped his Scotch as he admired the lights of this vibrant city he now called home. When he had moved to Singapore on transfer in early 2000, he had not planned to live here permanently. As much as his wife and children loved the cleanliness and the orderliness, Uday had found Singapore materialistic, unforgiving and soulless. It was just as his friends in India had described, and as he had read in various uncharitable reports about this city.

When his wife begged him to apply for citizenship a few years later, Uday was forced to admit that of the many places they had lived in before moving to Singapore, including London and Berlin, none had made him feel quite as safe, nor quite as successful, as this city. Not even Mumbai, where he was born and raised.

At the citizenship ceremony—a solemn event held at a community hall with a hundred and eighty other new citizens—Uday had sworn to be a good citizen. The guest of honour, a Member of Parliament, had urged the eager new citizens to be compassionate, to contribute to their new country and to build a society with character and competence. Uday and his family had no trouble living up to such expectations. His older son, Ashwin, had veered towards delinquency a few times in his teens, but National Service forced him onto the right track and he has since been a model citizen.

However, now, things had changed. Uday knew he was not a bad person; sometimes a man is forced to do one bad thing for the greater good. He downed the rest of his Scotch. He missed Julie, his late wife, terribly.

Uday settled into his favourite chair, a gift from his sons for his birthday—an Eames lounge chair and ottoman, the leather worn from providing years of comfort, and switched on his laptop.

Within an hour, he was convinced that he could orchestrate the perfect crime. Money buys everything these days.

Even absolution.

17

The Next Morning

Uday woke up to find Ashwin standing over him. Groaning as he sat up slowly, he asked, "What time is it?"

"Seven forty-five. You're going to be very late for work!"

"I've decided not to go in and have cancelled my meeting. I'll work from home all of this week."

"Good, because we have a lot to do and I'll need to be able to contact you all the time."

Ashwin sat at the edge of the bed, facing Uday, who propped himself against his pillow and three gaudy cushions Tamara had bought recently. Ashwin opened the pale green paper folder where a four-page report was punched and filed. On top of the report sat a plastic folder with a copy of the report, the pages held together with a paper clip. He handed the copy of the report to Uday. "I picked up this file ten minutes ago. It's from one of the best private investigators in Singapore. Thirty years with the police force, former Station Inspector. His son and I were in the army together.

"That was quick. When did you brief him?"

"Yesterday afternoon, between visiting Lavi, and coming over with what I'd found on Google search. It wasn't hard, considering we gave him photos and Shaun's work and home addresses. My friend's still digging up information. We're paying double for the urgency. I wish Sayana was here. I messaged him, but I don't think he can get away from his class. The first six pages are all about Shaun. She's a woman, Dad! Her real name is Sharon Lin Zhang Min."

Uday put on his reading glasses and glanced at a pixelated close-up shot of a spiky-haired young woman in a tank top and a leather choker, standing next to an older woman. Uday pulled the document closer and studied the picture of the older woman in huge sunglasses and long hair with curls cascading past her shoulders. He traced over the necklace she wore with his finger, a short, thin gold chain from which hung a stylised starfish. He handed the document to Ashwin, pointing at the older woman. "That ... that's Tamara—"

"No! Dad, surely not! The picture isn't very clear, so you can't be sure." Ashwin looked at the picture. "That doesn't look like Tamara. You're imagining things, Dad." Ashwin was holding a glass of water near his mouth. "Have a drink. Breathe slowly."

Uday pushed the glass away and stared at the ceiling. He spoke softly. "I'd recognise her even if she were cloaked in a *burqa*. That's definitely Tamara. That's the gold necklace and pendant I gave her soon after I started ... you know ... seeing her. Also, the more I see the picture of that vile spiky-haired creature, the more I recognise her as Tamara's daughter. I only met her once, briefly, when I was in Shanghai. I thought she looked familiar when I first saw the pictures on Sayana's phone, but I just couldn't process the information at the time, as Shaun was supposed to be a man."

Uday waved his finger as he pointed at the document. "It's them. Tamara and her daughter."

Ashwin shook his head. "I really don't think it's her. Her

floppy hat and sunglasses cover most of her face, but even so, looking at what's left to see, her lips look artificially plump—"

"That's what she calls her photo look, a skill acquired from when she was Miss Shanghai. She pouts, and it does look exaggerated, silly even, but she likes it. Don't bother studying the picture, Ashwin, it's her."

"I'm saying don't get so upset because I believe it's not her. I can think of a number of my friends with mothers who look similar. The ones we call *tai-tais,* the ladies of leisure. Immediately identifiable from the results of hours spent in the beauty salon, and a Filipina helper at their beck and call. The pendant is probably the most copied amongst Tiffany's designs. Lavi has one exactly like that in silver from a Bangkok street market and another that's gold-plated. Very common! By the way, why does Sharon look so Chinese? Wasn't Tamara's husband English? Her son Charlie looks mixed race."

"Sharon is Tamara's daughter from an assault by her father's friend. For the family to save face, Sharon was raised as Tamara's adopted sister. I'm not even sure Sharon knows the truth."

"She looks really ugly. But I still believe this isn't Tamara and her daughter. Besides, why would Tamara want to kill Lavi? Even if she had some bizarre reason, surely she'd expect you to find out?"

"If all had gone according to plan, whether hers or Sharon's, we'd never have found out. Lavi would be just another missing person and I'd be married to a devil woman."

Then Uday shuddered. Perhaps Ashwin was right. Perhaps he was imagining things. He was at such a loss as to who could have harmed Lavinia, refusing to believe Rohit could be spiteful to such a monstrous extent.

Ashwin flipped through the report while Uday lay in his

bed. "Sharon is suspected to be gay, which probably means the young girl with the bleached hair is really her girlfriend. There's something here about the restaurant where she works being owned by a relative. Sin Hoe Hin lists two Singaporeans and a Chinese national as directors. This one here sounds like a Chinese National's name—"

"How can you tell?"

"The other two names sound Singaporean Chinese. The older folks usually have dialect names. There's a Tan Kian Lian and Low Teck Wee. They sound like men's names. Do they mean anything to you?"

Uday shook his head.

"What about Wang Yan? Heard that name?"

Uday froze and shivered. He breathed rapidly before letting out a piercing wail. "It's her! That's Tamara's Chinese name! No! There's absolutely no more doubt! This is hundred percent proof, Ashwin!" Uday turned away from Ashwin and sobbed into his pillow. "Why? Why, why, why? What did Lavinia ever do to her to deserve this?"

"No, Dad, maybe not. It's a common name. A billion and a half people in China, even if one percent—"

"Ashwin, please! It's her! What more proof do you need? She planned it all. I'm a fool, such a fool!" Uday wailed. "Call Sayana."

Sayana took an early lunch break between his classes and drove to Uday's apartment. Uday had showered, shaved and was sitting in the upholstered fan-back armchair in his room. He sat with the bottom part of his right leg resting on his left thigh. He held his glass in his right hand—Baccarat crystal, one of a set of four which Julie had given him one Christmas—and ran his left finger along the perfectly cut patterns down the side. His composure betrayed the seething rage burning every organ, every cell, in his body.

Uday felt barbarous—in a somewhat pleasing way, if that were possible. Conjuring up her image sickened him. There was a time when he had adored Tamara, when all he had wanted was her. He could never have known what she was capable of. The beauty queen from Shanghai—intelligent, elegant and dainty—had morphed into a cunning, manipulative woman. Succubus personified, that's what she was.

He cursed the day he met her and heaped more curses on the day he proposed to her and insisted she move to Singapore as soon as she possibly could. How could he have been so blind to the signs, and allowed himself to be fooled? He had dismissed his children's suspicions as expressions of loyalty to their late mother. Now that he knew what really happened last night, Tamara Wang must pay for what she did.

Ashwin and Sayana sat next to each other at the foot of the bed, facing Uday.

"Boys, I want them both dead."

Sayana gasped. "Dad, you can't be serious. I know we said we'd handle this ourselves but we're not killers."

"I wouldn't be surprised if that devil woman arranged her husband's murder. I could be next."

Sayana shook his head. "No, Dad. We can't go around killing people. Let's just go to the police now. She'll be locked away. We'll all be safe!"

Ashwin turned to face Sayana. "You really believe that? Someone like her could harm us even from jail."

Uday's voice was flat and determined. "They must die."

"I want them dead, too. I'm sure we can arrange it," said Ashwin.

Sayana patted Ashwin on his back. "Yes, of course. You, my brother, are going to plan the perfect crime, I suppose?"

"No, *I* am." Uday took a big gulp from his glass of cold sugarcane juice. "Listen carefully. Imagine if all had gone according to plan—Lavi killed and burnt, her ashes flushed away like body waste, her unburnt bones dumped into a bin. Gone without a trace. No motive, no clues, no suspects, no evidence, no weapon, no body. Do you think the police would have solved the case?"

"Probably not," answered Sayana. "They would just keep Lavi on the missing persons list for seven years and then declare her dead."

"Rohit would still be a suspect, though," said Ashwin.

"For a day, that's all. They wouldn't be able to pin anything on him."

"Any updates on their investigations?"

Uday shook his head. "It's only been two days. Maybe they haven't been able to reach him, or maybe they need more time before contacting us with significant information." leaning back in his chair and with his palms together pointing in front of him, he repeated, "So, once again—no motive, no clues, no suspects, no evidence, no weapon, no body. The perfect crime. We're going to do something quite similar, but with a twist."

Sayana glanced at his watch. "I don't like where this is going, Dad. I don't want any part of this. Sorry, I have to run." Sayana stopped at the door and turned back, pulling out a piece of paper folded into four. "We should get security for Lavi, now that Tamara knows she's alive and Sharon is out there. I've got a shortlist of security agencies from a friend who runs a huge event management company. These fellows are used to protecting VIPs. There won't be guns, of course, but we should always have at least one guard in her room."

Uday nodded. "Go ahead, Sayana. I'd like twenty-four-hour protection for her, two guards at a time. It needs to be discreet. So far, we've been kept out of the news, so it looks like we can keep this quiet after all."

Ashwin whispered while Sayana was on the phone. "What about Sharon? Now that she must've heard from Tamara that Lavi's alive, we should at least try and keep her from trying to harm Lavinia or any of us. Security at the hospital will help, but who knows?"

Sayana announced that to avoid attention, one security guard was better than two, and he would be at the hospital in two hours. The hospital had been informed. Sayana made no effort to leave the room and sat on the bed while Uday spoke of his plans. "We'll start with Sharon and deal with Tamara later. She won't be back for another week. Call Sharon, Sayana." Uday handed him an old phone. "I use this for calls when I'm in Bali. Bought the SIM on the street. It can't be traced to anyone."

"Not a good idea. Sharon knows my voice. Ashwin should call her. Or you, Dad. Besides, if you're going to lure her to ultimately torture her, then I'm out of here. This is the point at which we should hand things over to the police. That's what you wanted to do in the first place, Dad. Go back to that plan. Justice, not vengeance." Sayana stood up, tossed the phone towards Ashwin and without another word, left the room, closing the door behind him.

Uday turned to Ashwin after Sayana left. "If you feel the same as your brother, that's okay. You can opt out if you wish. I'll get this done somehow."

"I'm in, Dad. Just very scared of something going wrong and us getting caught, but I feel vengeance is the only way we'll get justice for Lavi."

"We have to make sure it doesn't go wrong. Think of the thousands of crimes around the world that remain unsolved, not because of police incompetence—there's that, too, for sure—but mostly because someone didn't leave any trace. I hadn't realised it then, but throwing away those towels outside Dr Dubash's was just the beginning of doing things without leaving a trace. I now have a plan in mind, but I'd like to think about it for a while before discussing it with you."

Ashwin nodded and reached for the phone next to him. "I guess I should call her."

"She lives here. She must have picked up enough English to be able to understand what you want."

In a mock American accent, Ashwin asked, "Is this Sharon? Freelance chef?"

"Ya. You call from where? You speak Chinese?"

"Sorry, no, but I hope you can understand me. I'm calling from Indonesia, but I'm from Singapore."

"You speak slow slow, can? I no cook *ang mo* food. Chinese only. No free until April."

"Yes, Chinese food only. Tomorrow, Wednesday?"

"Tomorrow cannot! I working! Eh, your phone on speaker, is it? Why you do like that?"

"It's my father. He's on his computer and doesn't trust me to make the arrangements. He wants to listen, even if he's busy doing something else."

Uday smiled as he rolled his eyes and shook his head. "Hello, Miss Sharon!"

"Thing is, my father has very important guests from Jakarta and they only like Chinese food. They are rich and powerful people who don't want to be seen at restaurants. We thought a private chef would be perfect."

Sharon sighed and muttered under her breath. "Why so last-minute? Tomorrow cannot."

"I'm sure you can arrange a day off if I pay you extra?"

"If you want tomorrow, I must charge one thousand two."

Ashwin whistled. "What? A thousand two hundred dollars? That's four times your normal fee! I heard you charge three hundred per evening, excluding ingredients."

"That one last year. But I now best private chef to cook Chinese food, so my friend all tell me charge more. Now is six hundred. I still got many booking. You want me cook on off-day, you pay extra. You want or not?"

Ashwin glanced at Uday, who pursed his lips and nodded.

"Yes, we'll pay you a thousand two hundred."

"Okay. Tomorrow. I early morning come your house. Eight o'clock. We settle menu. You give me money, I go market. You SMS me where you stay."

Uday whispered to Ashwin and suggested a bus stop near a condominium several kilometres away.

"I'll pick you up at the bus stop outside Balmoral Plaza, along Bukit Timah Road. Be there at ten. Is that alright?"

"Late, but can. Also, cash only. No cheque, no bank transfer."

Uday felt victorious as Ashwin disconnected the call. "Now give me some time to think about my plan. Be back here in an hour."

18

Later That Morning

Uday handed Ashwin a four-page document, printed in monochrome on both sides and stapled.

"Whoa, is this a man or a woman?" Ashwin snickered as he took a second look at the picture of a woman with a masculine face and heavy make-up. She wore a bikini top barely holding up breasts too big for her frame, splashing in the sea. "Ah, it says here. Indonesian transgender killed by Australian husband. Oh dear. Poor thing."

"He was a chef. Cut her up and boiled her in chemicals. Neighbours complained about the stench and the police raided his place. He escaped and was found in a bin with a slit throat and a knife in his hand. Suicide, apparently. He got found out because he attracted attention with the foul smell. Stupid man, sloppy work, clearly unplanned. Happened late last year in Australia. Now go to page three."

Ashwin's eyes widened as he scanned the summary. "Six discharged in Curry Murder case. Not amounting to an acquittal." Turning to Uday, he asked, "Really? Curry murder?"

Uday spoke softly. "It goes back to 1984, when a woman reported her husband missing. Apparently, it had been six days since he had gone to Genting Highlands and not returned. The police filed a case of a missing person. A few months later, the wife took a job as caretaker of a church and moved into the premises with her three kids. Three years later, in January 1987, a police detective from the Criminal Investigation Department heard from a contact who insisted on meeting him to tell him face-to-face about a murder. They met at a quiet hawker centre where the contact told him about three men killing an Indian caretaker of an Orchard Road church—"

"The cute little white church across the street from Cathay cinema? A murder in a sacred place? Wow!"

"Yes, that one. The informant went on to say that the caretaker was chopped up and cooked in curry and rice before being disposed of in various rubbish bins. The constable was sickened by what he believed to be a tall tale, but the informant gave him the name of the victim and urged him to investigate his disappearance. Of course, when he returned to the CID and told his superiors what he had heard, they were sceptical. But as someone had come forward, the detective was required to conduct inquiries and to report to a senior policeman in the Special Investigation Section. The ball was rolling now!

The constable matched the victim's name with the one on the missing person report. He learnt that the victim was in debt, having borrowed six hundred dollars from his employer for his kids' books and school uniform. It was unlikely he would have gone to Genting Highlands, a gambling resort."

Uday flipped to the second page.

"That's a lot of information there, Dad."

"Yes, it'll take you too long to read the details, so I'm summarising the story for you. The policeman knew he was onto something and started digging. Within two weeks, he chased his first lead—a mutton seller at a market. Covert investigations continued. There was a team of senior officers on the case. They found three more suspects, two men and a woman. Within two months, the police got several teams to conduct an island-wide raid. They nabbed eight suspects—the victim's wife, her mother, her three brothers and their wives."

"The family must have hated him! I wonder why."

"There were reports that he had a terrible temper and was abusive, beating his wife regularly, especially when he had been drinking. The suspects were detained and questioned but it took two weeks before the police got any information. One suspect said the victim was bludgeoned to death with an iron rod at the Orchard Road church. Another suspect told the police that the victim was chopped into pieces and cooked in spices with rice. They then put the parts in bags and threw them in bins."

"Wow! I'd never imagine Singapore would have such gruesome criminals! How did you find this?"

"Didn't take long. I Googled 'Unsolved Murders Singapore.' About nine or ten came up. Most were violent. This was the most feasible one to copy."

"You can find more information on the internet when you're in the mood for something macabre. This, right now, is part of our plan. Just listen, okay?"

Ashwin rubbed his arms. "I'm getting goose bumps, Dad, but go on."

"The victim's widow and her three brothers, one of whom was the mutton seller, were charged with murder, which carries the death penalty. Their mother, and one of the brothers' wives, were charged with abetting the others in the murder. Two months later, on the day of their trial, the judge released all six of them—"

"No! Not with those confessions …"

"The prosecutor agreed he didn't have enough evidence. They had nothing but confessions, which were not enough for a murder trial. They got a discharge not amounting to an acquittal, which meant they could be tried on the same charges if new evidence surfaced. The day they were released, the three brothers were re-arrested under the Criminal Law Act and imprisoned for four years before being released. I don't have details on why they were re-arrested, but apparently the three challenged their imprisonment and were released unconditionally."

"They sound guilty as sin."

Uday shrugged. "Maybe they really were innocent, but I wouldn't be surprised if many people believed they were guilty. The point is, there was no evidence. We'll never know why the informant came forward, or how he knew about the murder. But if the six had kept the murder a secret, just between them, had they not been caught, had they not confessed, the dead man would still be just another name on a missing persons list. The key thing is to make absolutely sure we don't get caught."

"But what if …?"

Uday wagged his finger. "Not an option. Besides, you think anyone will bother making a missing person report against Sharon or Tamara?"

Ashwin smiled. "We're about to commit the perfect crime."

"Except we're not getting our hands dirty."

"But how, Dad? Do you know any church caretakers?"

"Not funny, Ashwin. I have some people in mind. For the venue, I think we should use your apartment."

"What? No! Angela would probably tip off the police. She can be so annoyingly self-righteous. As bad as Sayana. No, Dad. Please, not my place. Why not here? Sharon hasn't been here. She probably has no clue Tamara lives here. Has Tamara even mentioned Sharon since she arrived?"

"No. But Tamara may have told her where we live, the name of the condo. There's just one Rose Gardens."

"With more than two hundred apartments! This could be sheer coincidence."

"What about Conchita and Wati? We don't want them talking to a detective three years down the line. Plus, I have no idea when Aaron might be back. We don't want him walking in on us, do we?"

"That's easy, Dad. We'll just change the locks and have the management office deactivate his lift access card. As for Wati and Conchita, I can easily ask them to spend the day at our place, cooking and cleaning. I'll arrange it with Angela. She'd be delighted. Besides, they're never out here except for the mornings when Conchita's cleaning and in the evenings when they're serving dinner in the dining room. We'll use Charlie's room."

"We'll need the kitchen to cook. They can't be here until we're completely done, including cleaning up what will be a huge, disgusting mess, and are out of the flat. Also, there'll be a record of Sharon being here. Not that anyone would be looking for her, but just in case."

"Record? Seriously, Dad? Our security guards would let any of these six killers in, even if their faces were plastered all over today's papers. They're useless. They let every visitor's car or taxi through the barrier, they don't check which unit they're visiting, and they certainly don't bother filling out those little slips for people to place on their dashboards when using the visitors' carparks. I've heard that there are a few women who drop by regularly with their kids to use our pool. They don't even live here! Security here is a joke, Dad. All the more reason to get rid of Sharon before she gets rid of you."

"So, here's my plan and I need your help."

19

Uday stared at his breakfast. He barely touched the muesli Wati had perfected from a recipe Priyanka had given her some years ago. He fiddled with the little wooden teaspoon dunked in the matching bowl of *gula melaka* syrup. The thought of having to call Tamara while pretending all was well nauseated him.

Yet he needed to call Tamara. Besides he didn't want to agitate her when he probably had to lure her back within a few days. Uday picked up his phone. The children smiled at him from the screen. It was a picture taken last year while they were at Marina Bay. But he slid his phone into his pocket. He had no desire to start his day engaged in a conversation with the devil.

At nine in the morning, Ashwin called Uday to say he was meeting a man named Wilson, a real estate agent who had found tenants and buyers at Rose Gardens for the last fifteen years. According to Ashwin, landlords liked dealing with Wilson because he was personable, accessible and well-connected to the expatriate community.

"What's wrong with my place? Wati and Conchita plan to go over to your place soon. The coast will be clear all day."

"Too risky. Trust me on this, Dad."

"What makes you think Wilson will give you the keys?"

"I told him that you're having a party and we really only needed the space for the extra kitchen. He looked suspicious, but I told him that we were supposed to use my kitchen and yours, but Angela's pregnancy is making her sensitive to smells. He scrunched up his nose and nodded, said he understood, because Indian food really stinks. I wanted to thump him—"

"Still, why would he give you the keys? Why would he trust you?"

"He owes me, Dad. There are at least six tenants who are here because I recommended Wilson. Besides, the market is soft, and some apartments around here have been vacant for months. This one hasn't even had a viewing in two weeks. It's on the seventh floor, and the balcony faces the main road, so it's not easy to find a tenant. Too noisy. The landlord lives in Indonesia and refuses to lower the rent. Wilson won't get found out for letting me use it for a day, while putting a pretty decent amount in his pocket. Money for nothing, really. He's the exclusive agent, so no one else has the keys."

"It appears that you know too many people who are not exactly ... incorruptible."

"You know anyone who is?"

Uday breathed deeply. "Yes. Your sister and brother. Without a doubt. Must have taken after their mother."

Uday waited at the vacant apartment while Ashwin went to Serangoon Road to get what he needed—a large aluminium pot and charcoal burner, the same equipment as used by hawkers to cook biryani; curry powder; a large ladle which looked more like a paddle; and a pack of fifty oversized, extra-strong bin liners. He called Shaun to delay the pick-up time by half an hour.

There was a sofa and a dining table with six chairs, left behind by the previous tenant who did not want to ship them back to

England, and could not sell them before having to leave. The apartment was the same size and layout as Ashwin's and Sayana's, two bedrooms with en suite bathrooms. It was less than half the size of Uday's beautifully renovated four-bedroom apartment, all en suite, plus a powder room and a spacious utility area with a comfortable air-conditioned room for two domestic workers.

In contrast, this apartment was in its original condition, with all the bathroom and kitchen fixtures from the early nineties. It looked dated, with bathtubs, sinks and toilet bowls in hideous shades of pink, blue and yellow. Uday could not imagine a time when such fixtures were ever in vogue even in low cost housing. It baffled him that anyone, even back then, would have selected such colours for a luxury development.

Walking around the apartment, Uday noticed that all the rooms had windows facing towards other apartments. He could not see clearly through the open windows of other apartments because of the shadow, nor could he see through the closed windows because they were tinted and had highly reflective glass. Uday drew the curtains closed, only to realise that they were black-out curtains and there were no lights in the room. The previous tenants must have used floor or table lights; where there once might have been a pendant light hanging from a ceiling was now a fan. Uday went to his apartment and took the floor lamp from Charlie's room. After considering the logistics of all that needed to be done, he chose the second bedroom, seeing that it would be easier to clean it up. He switched on the air-conditioner, left the light on and closed the door behind him.

The flat was now ready to welcome Sharon. Uday sank into the plush velour sofa and checked his phone. Three missed calls and four text messages from Tamara. Uday snorted, before deciding it was best to send her a short message in the hope that she might stop calling. "Crazy day, darling. Going to be swamped with work all day and night. I'll call you tomorrow, okay?" Uday added the usual few emojis: heart, smiley face and cool guy.

Ashwin called from the car park at Rose Gardens to alert Uday that he was on his way. Uday dashed down to the fifth floor and pressed the lift call button. He jammed the door with a folded piece from a cardboard box, causing the lift to remain on that floor until he removed it. As soon as he heard Ashwin's deliberately slow, clunky footsteps from the stairwell, Uday released the cardboard bits and sent the lift back to the basement, where the carpark was.

Uday walked quickly back to the apartment and hid in the master bedroom, the door slightly ajar, in case Sharon recognised him from pictures Tamara might have shown her. It was fortunate that Ashwin did not look like Uday.

He heard Sharon huffing, puffing and cursing as she pulled out a chair and sat down.

"I'm so sorry that you had to walk up six floors. Every now and then, the lift seems to get stuck on the fifth floor. You must be so thirsty. I definitely need a drink. What would you like?"

"Water. No ice." She sounded like Tamara. It took months for Uday to get Tamara to say please and thank you, and she was still incapable of saying sorry. Now that he could see what Tamara was really made of, he was not surprised.

Ashwin yelled from the kitchen. "I have a lovely elderflower cordial. "Very nice, from England. Want to try some?"

"Okay. I try." Uday heard Sharon walking towards the balcony only to walk back to her chair. "Eh, why your flat so empty? Look like storeroom."

Ashwin spoke as he walked towards the dining table with

exaggerated heavy-footedness and placed Sharon's drink on the table. "My father's investment flat. For rental. We'll cook here but take the food to his apartment next door. It's going to be a big feast and the kitchen in his apartment is being used. You have everything here, utensils, stove, fridge and freezer … whatever you need for cooking. If there's anything else that you'd like, I'm sure you'll find it in my father's kitchen."

Sharon took several big gulps of her drink. "Okay. What you want to eat?"

"Firstly, thank you very much for coming over at short notice."

"You pay me, I come."

Uday flinched at her mercenary admission, delivered in the same frosty voice her mother had used yesterday.

"My father's paying. I can't afford a private chef," Ashwin laughed. "What are you planning to cook tonight? There'll just be the four of us: my father, his two business associates and me."

"My restaurant specialty suckling pig. I don't make myself but can get for you from special kitchen."

"No, thanks. No suckling pig. My father and I were thinking maybe a seven-course meal. Soup; roast pork belly; duck or chicken, braised; steamed fish; prawns, maybe cooked in a spicy sauce; shitake mushrooms; braised noodles and steamed rice. How does that sound? Do you have time?"

"Seven-course only? Normally Chinese meal is ten-course, minimum eight-course."

"Yes, we know, but our cook is also preparing a few dishes. Seven courses will be plenty."

"No problem but now quite late. You tell your maid help me. You give me three hundred dollars plus taxi money. I go market buy things."

Ashwin handed Sharon six fifty-dollar notes. "Here's three hundred. Please get a receipt from the stallholders." Ashwin noticed Sharon had not finished her drink. "Why don't you finish your drink? It's a hot day, you need to load up on liquid."

Sharon emptied the glass before standing up. She immediately held out her hand to balance herself.

"Are you okay, Sharon? You don't look well. Maybe you should sit down for a while."

Sharon nodded. "I … I okay. Must go market." She fell back down on her chair, placed her arm on the table, and her head flopped over her arm.

"Sharon?" Ashwin shook her shoulder. "Sharon? What's happened to you? Do you need to lie down?"

Sharon looked dazed. Slurring, she asked, "You have bed?"

Ashwin helped her to the second room and laid her on the floor. "No bed. This is more than you deserve."

Uday crept out of the master room and met Ashwin at the doorway. Ashwin snapped his fingers. "She's out, Dad."

"Are you absolutely, one-hundred percent sure? No chance of her waking up soon?"

"I mixed a little GHB—that club drug I told you about—and vodka into her water, which I flavoured with elderflower cordial. The guy I got the GHB from said vodka makes it more potent. Sharon would not have tasted the vodka. That was a really good idea, Dad, to have her climb part of the way. Anyone would need a drink after that."

"What time are your men coming?"

"I'll be picking them up at two. One of them only finishes work at one-thirty. The room is perfectly cold, so it's fine."

"What do you mean it's fine? They won't be here for three hours! What do we do until then?"

"We're going to need the time. Dad, think about this carefully. Are you sure you don't want to know about the two rapists and Sharon's yellow-haired girlfriend? Because if you do, we'll need time to get that information out of Sharon. But if you just want Sharon and Tamara dealt with, then we'll need to start soon."

Uday bored into Ashwin's eyes. "Yes, I just want Sharon and Tamara dealt with. Dead. Absolutely sure. How do you think we can exact revenge on the other three without entangling ourselves in the disappearance of Sharon and, in due course, Tamara? Are you so bloodthirsty before even committing your first crime?"

"You're right, Dad. Besides, as you'd mentioned last night, harming or killing them won't bring Lavi back to being the same young woman she was when she left home on Sunday afternoon."

"Especially as they were probably simple-minded lowlifes roped in by Sharon to do her dirty deed for compensation, which clearly would've come from Tamara. These two are the ones who should pay. With their lives!"

Ashwin nodded. "In that case, I'll have to get cracking. There's a time to kill and that time has come."

"What? No, Ashwin! You're not supposed to do the killing yourself. What's the point of hiring those two men?"

"Your suggestion to use migrant workers was excellent, Dad, but it's hard to go around making discreet enquiries about something like this. Seeing Lavi's condition deteriorating made me want to strangle those two myself. I wanted the pleasure of seeing in their eyes the same fear they must have seen in Lavi's eyes. I decided to ask for help just with the chopping, cooking and disposal. It was not as hard as I'd expected."

"I hope these men know exactly what they need to do. How did you find them, by the way? I mean, how did you know which man to approach?"

"I knew from my volunteer work with migrant workers that a number of them are holed up in makeshift shelters on the second and third storeys of those shophouses off Serangoon Road. Last night, I started at Cuff Road but no luck there. Tried a few other places as I walked down towards the temple. They're mostly decent fellows, out here to earn a living. There wasn't anyone whose situation was desperate enough for them to sell their souls to a devil like me. I found one of the men, Perumal, at a shelter along Desker Road. At around seven last evening, both sides of the street were teeming with men who seemed to be out of work. Some were on breaks, but according to Perumal, they had all lodged reports with the Ministry of Manpower and were waiting for their cases to be heard."

"What kind of reports? Were they injured? We read a lot about such cases. Too many, frankly, for a supposedly developed country."

"Many were injured, a few very badly. They were waiting for compensation and many were caught in salary disputes."

"Ah, yes, I've read about that, too. Unscrupulous employers who simply don't pay their workers' salaries for months and then declare bankruptcy. Bastards. May they burn in hell for an eternity! Fortuna has taken to task several sub-contractors for short-changing their workers."

"Perumal's employer hadn't paid him for seven months before filing for insolvency. Poor Perumal had borrowed six thousand dollars from rogue recruiters and they were hounding his family for payment. It's been tough for him, not sending money he had promised his family, and not paying back his loan.

"He's been waiting for three months to get something. His chances are slim, according to his social worker. The authorities tell him he must wait. He survives on charity and is desperate to go home, even if it means going back with no savings, in fact deeply in debt. When I offered him twenty thousand dollars, his face lit up. It was like watching fireworks going off in his head, blazing through his eyes. He clasped my hands and thanked me a million times, and started chanting some mantras softly, before asking me what I wanted him to do. 'What dirty work I do? You tell me, I do.' I swear, Dad. His exact words."

"So, he would've killed Sharon?"

"Yes. I am quite sure he would've if I had asked him to. I don't know about his friend, though. His name is Babu and he works as a butcher in Tekka Market. I asked him if he knew anyone willing to cut up a body. Perumal suggested Babu. His contract ends in a week and his employer refuses to transfer him to another employer. He'll be forced to return to India. He needs the money because one of his sisters is getting married and another just started high school this year."

"You'll be picking them up and driving them here?"

"Yes." Ashwin stood up and walked towards the room where Sharon lay on her back, looking as if she was sound asleep. "I need to start the … you know …"

Uday followed closely behind. "I'm glad we didn't use any of our apartments for this. I wouldn't want the extermination of evil to take place in our own home." Uday shivered and rubbed his arm. "Why the need for sub-arctic temperature?"

"We need her body to be dead for about two hours before they cut her up. Less blood apparently. The longer the better, but we don't have much more time. Keeping it cold during that period prevents it from rotting. Learnt this by searching online. I went to an internet café, by the way. No one cared about identification. Left no trace."

Ashwin dragged Sharon from one end of the room to the

other and raised her upper body, before releasing her onto the wooden floor with a thump. Ashwin patted her face, hard enough so it sounded like a slap. "Oy, Sharon! Wake up!"

"Isn't that drug supposed to knock her out for hours?"

"Yes, but I gave her a very light dose, enough just to make her sleep for a while but not enough to knock her out completely." Ashwin stood in front of Uday, unusually close, and said in a voice and tone Uday had never heard him use, "I want her to know what is going to happen to her. I want her to feel what I am going to do."

Uday wasn't sure if he wanted to watch. He stared at Sharon, her body curled up on the floor, her eyes struggling to open, muttering in Chinese. Nightmare visions of what she had done with the help of the hooligans she had recruited and paid swirled through his head.

"Do what you want to do, Ashwin. Let me know if I can help."

Ashwin splashed some water on Sharon. She coughed and tried to sit up.

In a soft voice, just above a whisper, Sharon struggled to speak. "Who are you? Why you do this?"

Ashwin threw his head back and laughed. He kicked her thigh. "I am Lavinia's brother, you piece of shit." He stretched his hand out towards Uday. "Please meet Lavinia's daddy."

Sharon tried to stand. Ashwin pushed her down with one hand on her shoulder. "You're not going anywhere. You're going to get everything you did to my sister and much more."

Sharon's eyes widened, and she put her hands together. She could barely speak and looked as if she was about to faint. "Sorry. Very sorry. Please. Please ... you no harm me. Please! My mama tell me do, tell me kill Lavi. Sorry, sorry ..." Sharon collapsed on the floor and sobbed.

Ashwin looked at Uday and smiled. "The confession. She knows Tamara is her mother. Even better." Ashwin took two pairs of handcuffs from his bag. He sat at Sharon's feet as she tried to pull away. Her limbs flailed weakly, making it effortless for Ashwin to lock the handcuffs around her feet and wrists. Uday had meant to help him but found himself bolted to the doorway.

"Here's the story of the next and last ten minutes of your life." Ashwin sat cross-legged on the floor and faced Sharon. He raised her chin so he could look into her eyes. She turned away. "First, I am going to strangle you with my bare hands. You will be looking at me as I see the life fizzle out of you. It will be slow. I promise." Ashwin clenched his fist and released it, repeating the cycle several times. "Very slowly." Sharon's breathing became more rapid, her nostrils flared and she started crying.

"You're crying? Tears of fear? Anger at your mother for getting you into this? The mother who was so ashamed of you, she pretended you were her adopted sister?" Sharon pulled her face away from Ashwin and buried her face into her knees. "I'm so sorry. I hurt your feelings, did I? Did you think for a second how Lavi's family felt when she didn't show up for dinner? How we felt when we found her on that table? How we feel every minute of the day, wondering if she'll make it through? We found her only because Ah Huat got greedy. If not, we'd have no idea where Lavi was and she would never be found." Ashwin slapped Sharon. "Don't you show me those crocodile tears!"

Uday felt his stomach churning. Despite the viciousness this creature had inflicted on his beloved Lavinia, Uday couldn't bear to watch Ashwin bring her life to a gruesome end. "Ashwin, this is too much for me—"

Ashwin walked towards his father and whispered in Hindi, "Have you changed your mind, Dad? I can release her if you want me to. We'll call the police instead."

Uday glanced at Sharon lying prone on the floor. He waved his hand in front of him. "I haven't changed my mind, but I don't want to watch. I'll be at the hospital. Call me when you're done. I'd like to be here when the two men arrive. I feel a pressing need to vet them before trusting them with this despicable deed."

20

The Same Afternoon

Ashwin turned up with the two men later than scheduled, at 4pm. Leaving them in the living room with Uday, he dashed into the second room where Sharon lay, to check that all the items the men needed were in place.

Uday smiled as they greeted him with the traditional Hindu greeting, hands together as if in prayer, saying *namaste*. Uday couldn't help but wonder about the stripes of yellow and grey ash on their foreheads. "Did you just go to the temple?"

The burly man, Perumal, probably in his forties, with a thick mop of hair stained red with cheap henna dye, spoke English quite fluently but with a heavy accent. "Must pray, Sir. God give me luck, now I go home. I have money."

The other, known as Babu, a diminutive fellow with a nose too bulbous for his bony face, who looked no older than twenty, barely understood anything except Tamil. He was carrying a bag far too big for his slight frame. Uday shuddered to think what was in there; how many people wandered around the city with lethal weapons in their bags? Standing next to each other, they looked like an Indian adaptation of Asterix and Obelix. Uday tried not to laugh. Speaking slowly and softly, he asked, "Do you know why you're here?"

Ashwin bellowed from the other room in Hindi. "I've already made it clear, Dad. The more you ask them the more they're going to think about it and might just change their minds."

Uday ignored him.

Perumal, the burly one, nodded and handed both their passports to Uday. "Your son say you keep passport. When we finish work, you give back passport. Also give plane ticket and some money."

"Yes. A lot of money. Tell me what you're supposed to do. I just want to be sure you know what is expected for the amount I am supposed to pay you."

Perumal translated Uday's conversation to Babu, who spoke in Tamil as he rotated his head in agreement. Looking directly at Uday, Perumal said in a voice and tone so cold it could instantly freeze the warm air stirred by the fan in the living room. "We chop one man, already dead—"

"A woman, actually."

Perumal gulped, leaning forward and frowning as he asked, "Woman? I don't know, sir. No good to do this type of bad thing to woman."

Uday pursed his lips and looked away. He sighed as he turned back to Perumal and said, "She is not really a woman. She is the devil incarnate. She tried to kill my child. She wanted my child chopped and burnt. You should not feel badly about her just because she's a woman. Now, please continue with what you'll need to do."

"First, we chopping, after finish chopping, we cooking, use curry powder—" At the sound of the words, "curry powder", Babu giggled and shook his head, rotating it as if in agreement. Perumal continued, "After finish cooking, put in different different bag, then you take us by car to many many place, then we throw bag different different dustbin. Correct sir?"

"Correct. Except I won't be driving you. My son will do that."

Uday got up, told the men to wait for him and walked to the bedroom, where he had last seen Sharon.

Ashwin had just finished lining the floor with tarpaulin, held down in the centre by two wide wooden planks placed side by side, each the size of a rectangular four-seater dining table. Sharon lay still, her back towards the wall below the window. The room was freezing.

Ashwin stood up and hugged his father. "All set, Dad. In a few minutes, the most gruesome part of our plan will be executed."

Shaking his head and rubbing his face, Uday whispered, "I can't believe—"

"It was your idea, Dad. You planned it, asked me to recruit the men. I did that. What are you saying now?"

"I'm just ... I suppose I didn't expect you to do it. To kill."

"I know. Nor did I. The intensity of my desire for revenge shocked me."

They both stood silent for a while and stared at Sharon's body.

"What have I become, Dad? My soul, my mind, they are gnarled in turmoil. I watched her gasp and writhe until her body went still. And then I ... I ... smiled. After doing something so nefarious, a pleasurable feeling washed over me. Something so perverse and so pure at the same time."

Uday put his arm around Ashwin. "I'm sorry you had to be the one to do this. Thank you. You have avenged a most heinous crime against your sister." Uday stared at the stiff body on the floor, arms and legs straight and as stiff as the planks next to it. "The men are waiting for you. You picked them well. The little one seems especially ruthless."

"You should leave, Dad. Go home. I'll take care of this. I've got everything I need, including the cleaver, two large aluminium pots, two large charcoal burners, bags of curry powder and at least fifty heavy-duty bin liners ..."

Uday shook his head and turned away.

Uday wasn't sure whether to feel proud of his son for taking control, or disgusted by the ease with which he believed Ashwin carried out the murder and was about to oversee the elimination of evidence.

For the love of someone, he had said. Uday understood. He did not hide his relief when he towered over Sharon's dead body. As he walked towards the lift, Uday clutched his chest. Was that the sting of deep, black ink seeping into his heart, swallowing his soul? Or immense relief masquerading as guilt?

21

Uday is spending some time with Lavinia this afternoon. Earlier, the doctor told him that Lavinia's condition is deteriorating. Her heartbeat and blood pressure are dangerously low. Her responses to the eye, motor and verbal tests suggest that her chances of a full recovery are slim. When the doctor told Uday all this, I realised I had been imagining things—Lavinia has neither opened her eyes nor spoken to me since she was hospitalised. It is amazing what a mother chooses to believe when she is desperate.

I thought the doctor should have been more forthright with Uday, like when he told the medical students—the same group who visit every morning—that Lavinia was unlikely to get any better and was very likely to die within weeks. But I suppose it's hard to tell a hopeful father his beloved daughter is not going to make it. Easier to string them along for a while. Perhaps make it look like the doctors did their best.

I have never seen Uday so distraught. He asks the nurses and doctors to leave him alone for some time. He wants to talk to Lavinia in private. The nurses are kind, they nod and smile and assure him they understand.

Uday tells Lavinia that her attacker was not a boy, but a woman named Sharon. Ashwin is doing what he has to do. Uday weeps as he holds Lavinia's hand and tells her that it was his idea, that he could see no other way to get justice for what Sharon did to her. He does not tell Lavinia exactly what is happening. Just that Sharon is dead and they will no longer have to worry about Lavinia or anyone in their family being hurt. I take that to mean that Ashwin has killed Sharon, and Uday was part of it.

There is no mention of Sayana. Either they kept it from him— for all his smart aleck ways, he was always remarkably righteous— or he refused to be part of it. I can't be sure. Like Sayana, Lavinia is a good person, the kind who would rather guide a cockroach to finding its way out than kill it with bug spray. Lavinia would probably not want to know her brother killed someone, even if that monster had no compunction abducting innocent Lavinia and trying to get her chopped up and burnt to cinders.

Uday stares at Lavinia for a long time. I don't know what he is thinking. I stand behind him and put my arms over his chest as I wrap myself around him. He flinches for a moment, and then settles. He leans back against his chair and closes his eyes, breathing deeply. I tighten my arms around his shoulders and tell him that Ashwin and he are doing the right thing. I thank him. He raises his right hand and pats his chest. I think he means to pat my arm. He feels me. He knows I am with him.

"It was Tamara," whispers Uday. I don't know if he is talking to me or to Lavinia. Maybe to both of us. It doesn't surprise me. After everything Lavinia told me about her, I expected an insecure bitch like Tamara to be jealous of Lavinia. "She's next."

I take that to mean Tamara will also be killed. No, I shall not have my son kill someone for whom a far more appropriate punishment would be a cell in Changi Prison for life. I watched her from the moment she moved in. Always looking in the mirror. Admiring her reflection every time she passed by a panel of reflective glass, from the picture frames which adorn virtually every wall, to the floor-to-ceiling balcony doors. She was never without make-up except when she was about to slide into bed and when she woke up in the morning. She always rose before Uday, got showered, dressed and dolled up. No wonder he called her his China Doll.

I, on the other hand, never even wore lipstick or mascara, but ever since I met Uday, he made me feel like the most beautiful woman in the world, like the only woman who ever really mattered to him. I was his English Rose. It's why he insisted on buying an apartment in Rose Gardens, even though we could not afford it at the time.

Back then, Uday had said, "It's for you, my English Rose. We'll just have to drive a modest car, take fewer and shorter overseas holidays, eat at home most of the time ... we'll manage."

The self-centred *tai-tai*, as she likes to call herself, is all about comfort. I think she genuinely believes that a life of luxury was her right, and is her right, rather than a privilege. She is shameless, pestering Uday to buy her expensive jewellery and wine and dine her at lavish restaurants. He succumbed to almost every whim of hers, but that's over now.

I whisper in his ear, and blow my words deep, deep inside. *Jail for Tamara. Worse than death.* Uday flinches, rubs his ear, as if trying to get rid of an itch inside. I want to say, yes, my love, I am your itch. This Indian Rose has sharpened her thorns but only to protect you.

Uday looks around, puzzled. He stares at Lavinia, his breathing slow and deep. He buries his face in Lavinia's hand. Poor fellow. It pains me to see him in such a state. "She was the puppet-master. She must be punished severely." Uday spits out those words.

He just sits and stares at Lavinia. At about six thirty, he gets a message. Ashwin is ready. Uday is unsteady as he stands. He supports himself with the help of the side bar on Lavinia's bed and leans forward to kiss her. "Lavinia, light of my life. May you wake up soon."

He hesitates before stroking her face and stammers, "I … I love you, Lavi, light of my life." Uday finds it hard to say those three words. I love you. He used to say that it was a Western thing. How could a husband and wife not love each other? How could parents not love their children? When I told him that saying "I love you" was merely an affirmation, he said if people were so easily affirmed by words used so freely, then those were cheap words. Uday hardly ever told me he loved me, and never told the children that he loved them. But I know he loved me, and still does, and I know he loves his children with all his heart, his soul, his very being.

It is nearly seven in the evening when Uday finally gets up to make his way home. He runs his fingers through Lavinia's hair, apologising for having to leave. He has things to do, he says. Things he must do for her and her brothers' sakes. Uday stands at the window, which faces west. The sky is brilliant shades of blue and pink, rippled with clouds which look like clusters of tiny cotton puffs in row upon random row. I put my arm around his waist and together, we admire the soft colours of the evening sky. He does not flinch, not like he did earlier. He turns towards me, then looks back at Lavinia and smiles.

He knows. He must know I am here.

22

Uday walked down the hospital corridor, thinking about the grisly scene awaiting him at the apartment. As he approached the lift, he felt giddy and nauseous. He stretched out his left hand to support himself against the wall. He grimaced as he turned his face against his shoulder.

A nurse walking past Uday stopped and asked, "Sir, are you alright? Sir?" She was petite, and twisted her body and neck to try and look at him. "Oh! You are Miss Lavinia's father. Please, sir, I think you should take a seat." She pointed towards a sofa a few metres away.

"Thank you. I think it's just … low blood pressure." Uday leant back. He was not ready for the task of dumping garbage bags around the island. He wanted to stay with Lavinia.

The nurse brought him some warm water in a slightly chipped melamine mug. He hated the taste; it needed a slice of lemon to make it drinkable. It would be rude to ask for anything to flavour the water with, and even more rude not to drink at least some of it. Uday drank half, placed the mug on the table and waved his thanks to the nurse. What he really needed was a cold drink, ideally a Scotch on the rocks.

Uday's phone rang as he waited for the lift. "I'm just leaving.

It's too soon, anyway. Weren't we going to start at ten?"

"Yes, but these two forgot their luggage so I'm going to drop them off somewhere close by, have them take a taxi to their place, then pick them up later. I just thought we could have dinner together."

"I ... I don't feel like eating. I could use a stiff drink though. See you at the flat in about half an hour?"

"Dad, meet me at the car park of this block. Everything's done. I got a suitcase from my place and the two stuffed it with bin liners filled with ... what do we call them ... remains? Much easier for transporting them. It seemed like a good idea to put those bits and pieces into a suitcase and wheel them to the car, rather than to carry bags that might still smell of curry."

The image made Uday gag. He took a deep breath. "I'll call you as I drive in to Rose Gardens."

Uday looked for his car. It took several seconds before he remembered he had driven to the hospital in a rental car. It had been decades since he'd driven a Japanese model. He had hired a silver Toyota, a common car which would not raise any suspicion, while he drove three men around the island, on their mission to dump garbage bags filled with gory contents. To avoid all suspicion, Uday had asked his chauffeur to send his BMW for servicing that morning and given him the day off.

As he drove away from the hospital, Uday observed the rubbish bins. Ashwin was right; they were identical all over Singapore—tall, green vertical bins for houses and deep, wide bins for buildings, including condominiums. Ashwin had mapped out the seven waste collection zones and the four collection points which served them. Uday braced himself for a long night. The plan was to drop a bag into a waste bin at each of four different zones. A fifth bag would be thrown into the sea, weighed down with stones.

Ashwin buzzed Uday up the lift. "I thought you were going to call, and I would meet you downstairs."

"I forgot." A large soft-top suitcase stood by the door. It smelt faintly of cinnamon and curry. Uday tried to lift it. "At least fifty kilos, I'd say. Grossly overweight."

Ashwin laughed. "Only for checked-in luggage. She was grossly underweight. But very strong."

Uday walked towards the kitchen. "Just want to make sure the whole flat is perfectly clean, without a trace of what happened."

"All clean. I checked. Those two did a good job. They were so efficient, even took their clothes off—"

"Naked?"

Ashwin nodded. "Almost. They covered themselves in plastic sheets. At one point, I wondered if they'd done this before. Especially that little one, Babu, whom I found smiling several times as he packed the suitcase. It was disturbing. I wish I hadn't watched—"

"You watched it? Why?"

"It was grotesque yet also fascinating in a twisted way. But I wouldn't want to make a sport of it. Besides, I gave up early on. I just couldn't ..."

Uday shook his head as he remembered Ashwin's childhood obsession with horror movies. Today, Ashwin had unwittingly starred in his very own private production, with visuals which would probably continue to re-surface in his mind.

Satisfied that the kitchen was clean, Uday walked to the bedroom. He picked up the lamp from the floor and thrust it at Ashwin. "How could you forget this? Evidence!"

"Sorry, Dad. I didn't realise it was ours. I don't remember seeing it at home."

"It was in Charlie's room. Used to belong to Sayana."

"Ha! Whether he liked it or not, a part of him was watching everything! I should tell him that."

That leap of logic was alien to Uday. "You'll do no such thing. The poor fellow is probably already traumatised about what we're doing. There's no need to torment him any further. I'll have you know that Sayana hated that lamp. Thought it was too ugly and old-fashioned. He only kept it because he was with your mother when she bought it from a vintage shop."

Uday helped himself to a Scotch after it was agreed that Ashwin would drive. "Change of plans, Dad. Perumal suggested we only dump the bags in those big bins at hawker centres, markets and restaurants. He said that rubbish collectors in residential zones lift bags out of bins by hand—"

"What? They stop outside every house, lift the bin covers and remove the bags by hand?"

"Yup, and then they hurl them into the rubbish truck. I've seen them do this, but never gave it much thought. There can't be that many bags in the bins, considering they're cleared every day, even on Sunday."

"How are the big bins cleared?"

"They're wheeled out to the truck, then slotted into levers at the bottom of the truck, which then lift the bin and tip all the contents into the truck. Much safer for us to use those bins."

Uday nodded as he sipped his Scotch. "Still planning to go all over the island?"

"Not quite all over but several places, quite spread out. I didn't have much time to choose the places, but I know at least six hawker centres that close early and are deserted by 9pm. And, of course, many have markets close by. They're dead by four in the afternoon. For now, I'm planning on going to Jurong, Bukit Batok, Changi and Beach Road."

"I'm glad you're driving!" Uday glanced at his watch. "We have about half an hour before they call, and we'll need to leave to pick them up. Tell me what happened after I left."

Ashwin looked away. "It was gruesome. Why would you want to hear about something when just an hour ago you wondered why *I* watched?"

Uday stared straight ahead. "I don't know. I wanted this to happen, yet didn't want to be an active participant. Seeing Lavi today ... I don't know how much longer ... I don't know, Ashwin." Uday breathed slowly and deeply. He pursed his lips and faced Ashwin. "In some primeval way, I now feel the need to remember that every stage of her ordeal was filled with violence, humiliation and indignity. No matter how much was dished out, nothing can ever make up for what was heaped upon our beloved Lavi. Now, go on, tell me what the men did."

Ashwin turned to face his father. Eyebrows furrowed, he asked, "Are you sure, Dad?"

Uday took a deep breath and nodded slowly. "Yes. I want every detail. Just don't say her name."

Ashwin took a deep breath and leant back into his seat. "I'll never regret what I did. Even if our precious Lavi does get better by some miracle. So, you sure you want me to tell you the details?"

"Yes. Go on."

"After you left, I knelt in front of her and promised her that her mother will die, too. More slowly, more painfully. But before that, I would throw a banquet for her mother. I squeezed her skinny thigh and said, "we'll be making some juicy koftas from here." She was horrified, Dad. She stamped her cuffed feet and tried to scream, but her mouth was taped. I said I'd take some meat from here, mince it, mix it with minced lamb and we'd make special *koftas* just for her mother. After her mother had eaten a few mouthfuls, we'd tell her what she ate—"

Uday covered his mouth with both hands and inhaled. "Oh, Ashwin! I hope you weren't serious."

"Sorry Dad, I know it's sickening. It was a joke. I have no intention of doing that. Too repugnant even for me!"

"No more of the grisly details. Just tell me one more thing— how did her life end? Was there pain?"

"There was some pain, Dad, but nothing like what Lavi must have suffered. Remember, the doctor said Lavi's gash was so deep that he could see her cheekbone, and the slash went right through her cheek, into her mouth? They took ages to stitch up Lavi's face. I wanted to do the same to this monster but all I could manage was a small cut with a fruit knife on one side of her face. She barely flinched."

"That's hardly any pain for someone with tattoos all over her body! So, how did her life end?"

"Just as I had promised her. I got a pair of latex gloves and straddled her. I squeezed both my hands around her neck. After twenty seconds, I released my grip. She convulsed throughout. I repeated this cycle five or six times, and then I kept my grip steady for over a minute, until she went still. After two minutes, she still had a very faint pulse. So I clamped her head and—"

"Alright, enough. Now I know how she died. Probably from strangulation, but to be sure, you broke her neck." Uday bit his knuckles. "What have we done, Ashwin?"

"We've just avenged the attack on Lavi, part one. We're not done yet."

23

Later That Night

The car park at Rose Gardens was quiet, residents comfortably ensconced in their homes, winding down for the day. All the parking lots were filled with cars, mostly luxury brands in sumptuous colours of 21st century paint, with names like Imperial Metallic Blue and Celestial Black, upholstered in colours like Caramel Nappa. His rented Toyota Vios in silver with black synthetic interiors looked and felt austere in comparison.

From where he stood, a few feet away from the glare of the fluorescent tube light on the ceiling, Uday looked beyond the car park exit towards the shrubbery. A number of foreign domestic workers were chatting while walking their employers' dogs. It reminded Uday of his last attendance at the condominium's annual general meeting, where, for the last six years, he had asked for surveillance cameras, to prevent people from allowing their dogs to urinate and defecate near the lift lobby. Clearly, some people lacked civic consciousness and needed to be watched or caught, he regularly implored. Every year, the management committee, with barely suppressed smugness, thanked him for his views, and every year they said they would look into it, a euphemism for focussing on other matters. Tonight, he felt beholden to that smug group of people for being so unwelcoming towards his suggestions, those men who drove their super cars and lived in multi-million-dollar apartments, the same men who pretended to serve residents and care for their condominium while wanting to continue wielding power outside their offices.

Uday jumped, and put his hand to his chest when Ashwin tapped him on his shoulder. "Hey, Dad! Help me with these, please."

The whiff of freshly roasted cinnamon bark greeted Uday and Ashwin as soon as they opened the boot.

"That's not her natural smell, for sure," whispered Uday, as he looked around to ensure no one else was in the carpark.

Ashwin whispered back. "Perumal's idea. He brought several packets, about thirty sticks altogether. Roasted them before throwing a few in each bag. No matter how well the bags are tied and sealed with tape, some smells do escape. Better the fresh aroma of cinnamon than that." Ashwin pointed to the five bags lying in the suitcase. "There are several other sticks strewn around in here. Must remember to clear them before we return the car."

Ashwin unzipped the suitcase and handed two of the lightest bags to Uday. "We'll put them all in the back seat, with Perumal and Babu. Space will be tight, but I can't see that the men would mind holding them until they're dumped. Saves us from unloading the suitcase again."

Uday wasn't sure if he wanted to know which parts he was carrying. They were all so well-padded with reams of newspapers that it was hard to tell between a quarter of a torso and a few chunks of limbs piled together. All he could think of as he held the bags was how much Sharon deserved to meet such a disgusting end. As he laid the bags on the rubber rugs of the car floor, he felt convinced that imprisonment would be more gruelling for a woman like Tamara Wang. He would torment Tamara by narrating the horrors of Sharon's last hours by describing them to her in graphic detail. He could neither put Ashwin, nor himself, through yet another killing.

The men were waiting with their luggage—two small suitcases each, containing all their worldly belongings and memories of Singapore—when Ashwin pulled up outside a money remittance shop along Buffalo Road. They wore black clothes and black shoes, as agreed earlier that evening. It made them less visible in dark places. Perumal had joked that it was fortunate that he and Babu had very dark skin, to add to their invisibility. Ashwin didn't think it was funny but appreciated the reality.

A few men were packing up their flower stalls across the road. Ashwin had just driven off when, in the distance, Uday saw six wide bins, the same as the ones used at hawker centres. "Stop, Ashwin!" Pointing to the bins in the shadows, Uday said, "There! We could dump one bag in that bin. It's behind a market so there's nothing but food waste, especially raw meat and fish bones. The cooked pieces will be right at home in there, I'd say."

Perumal leant forward, thrusting his head between their seats. "No, sir. Cannot put anything here. After big riot in Little India, many, many camera now in here area."

Uday stiffened and turned to Ashwin, "Cameras. Us picking up these two has been caught on camera?"

Ashwin pointed to a lamp post as they drove past. "That's where the camera is, pointing towards the taxi stand. It's why Perumal asked me to pick him up from back there. If not for the cameras, those bins would be ideal. I found out that market bins get cleared first thing in the morning," said Ashwin. "Heading west now. We'll be at our first stop in half an hour."

Uday cringed at the rustling of the plastic bags as the two men buckled up their seat belts. He tried to picture the contents.

Turning to Ashwin, he asked in Hindi, "You said earlier that you watched some of it ... the chopping. Tell me what you saw."

Ashwin glanced at Uday. "Dad, what's the matter with you? You really don't want to know. Once you hear it, you'll never be able to un-hear it. It'll be in your mind, with images you'll inevitably create as I narrate what happened."

"I know. Tell me. In Hindi. No need to use their names. Big and Small will suffice."

Ashwin pursed his lips and reduced his cruising speed. "Those two decided the shower stall was best for cleaning up the mess. First, they dressed themselves in sheets of plastic and put on latex gloves. Then they removed the handcuffs from her wrists and ankles, undressed her and carried her limp body to the bathroom. They placed it in the shower stall, which was a good size but not large enough for three of us. Small put the body in a sitting position and pulled the shower curtain way back, while Big stood just outside, near the loo, holding the plastic bag in which he would put the parts. Small took a cleaver from his backpack and dug into that bit between the thigh and pelvis. It seemed to come apart quite easily, without him having to chop it with force. It looked like he sliced it off, tugging a bit here and there. I gagged when he pulled her leg apart. I couldn't watch anymore, so I left the bathroom but stayed in the room, sitting against the wall under the window, listening.

"Big provided a rather good commentary as he watched. Once the legs were gone, Small laid her on the floor and sliced off her arms. The limbs were stacked on one side of the shower. They were too stiff to bend so he had to prop them up against the wall. Small then placed a plastic chopping board under her head and removed her head. I heard the crack as soon as Big said it was going to happen. Big said Small was about to halve the torso.

At that point, I walked out of the room and said I didn't want to hear those details. Organs spilling out and all ... Eeeewwww!" Ashwin gagged. "As I closed the door, I asked Big to call me when he was done."

"Wise. The most vile images and sounds can neither be unseen nor unheard." Uday rolled the window down. He was both repulsed and soothed by Ashwin's narration.

"Shall I go on, Dad?"

Uday nodded.

"After the torso was quartered, Small used an electric cutter—a cylindrical saw, quite a cool gadget—to cut the limbs into several pieces. I heard it grinding through the bone. For some parts, he used a cleaver to chop her up. It was quite loud, and I was worried one of the neighbours might come around and ask questions, but it was over in less than ten minutes. Small was amazing!"

"How many pieces?"

"Big told me Small first severed the feet and then sliced the legs into two, separating them at the knees. Then he hacked the lower legs into four pieces each, and the thighs into eight, halving them vertically at the upper thighs." Ashwin counted on his fingers, tapping on the steering wheel before stopping to do mental sums.

"Twenty-six. You're a bit slow today."

Ashwin sulked. "Like the legs, the hands were severed before the arms were sliced into two at the elbows. Then the upper arms were cut into four and the forearms into three. That would be—"

"Sixteen."

"Yes. A lot of pieces, all dumped into rubbish bags. When they were done, Big and Small went into the kitchen with three bags—one with the limbs, the other with the torso and the last one with the head. They asked for the pots and pans. I showed them the huge aluminium pot, paddle and charcoal burner, like the ones supposedly used in the curry murder case. Big suggested we use smaller pots, as it would be quicker and more efficient, ensuring the parts were evenly cooked. Raw flesh would rot quickly and stink even through well-sealed bags. He also said the charcoal burner takes too long to heat up and might release too much smoke. He preferred to cook on the stove. There weren't any pots in the kitchen, so I went to your flat and got four of the biggest pots I could find. I put them in those extra-large, blue bags we had lying around and lugged them back.

"They boiled four pots of water, one on each gas burner, and poured generous amounts of curry powder into each pot. Wait, I said, aren't you first supposed to fry the pieces in oil, before adding the liquid? Big laughed and said, yes, if you're cooking meat to eat, in which case you would first fry onions, garlic and ginger before adding the curry powder and the meat. He was boiling the meat to prevent the flesh from rotting quickly. Still laughing, he asked if we were planning to eat her. Not funny, I said, it's just that I'd watched Wati cook curry many times. He apologised. The kitchen smelt of curry powder, but considering how much was used, it was not as strong as when Wati cooks curry. I'm sure frying intensifies the fragrance and taste. It certainly wasn't aromatic."

"Did it stink? The flesh?"

"Not that I could discern. There was a smell of flesh cooking, but it could have been beef or pork. I don't know. I smelt mostly curry powder. He cooked the parts in three batches, each batch taking about twenty minutes. The water took a while to boil, but the flesh itself seemed to cook quickly, according to master chef Big. It was all over in less than ninety minutes."

Uday pursed his lips, unsure if he really wanted the answer to the question he was about to ask. "The head? How did he cook that?"

"Big said he placed the whole head in the deepest pot—a stockpot, I think—which was just deep enough to cover it with water. It was the last thing he cooked, so while I saw all the other pieces spread across the floor, I never saw the head. I couldn't bear to. I guess I knew I would never be able to get the image out of my head."

"And seeing the other pieces?"

"Strangely, I felt nothing. It struck me as odd at the time, but now, telling you about it, it feels almost cathartic. Like ridding our family of an evil presence."

"The real and absolute evil force is Tamara."

Ashwin shrugged. "Yup, and we'll do what we must. Do you want to hear the rest of it?"

Uday thought he'd heard everything. He wasn't interested in the other details but Ashwin seemed keen to fill him in. "Go on, then."

"It took another hour for all the pieces, spread out on stacks of newspapers on the floor, to cool completely. I had bought several copies of Chinese papers at various shops. If ever, through sheer bad luck, a rubbish bag is found—"

"That is never an option in a perfect crime. You simply don't get into that situation."

"Yes, Dad, I know, but just in case, then the police would immediately assume the killers are Chinese. Throws them off the trail. Besides, there'll be no other evidence, or a motive." Ashwin tapped his temples and smiled. "Good thinking on my part, right, Dad?"

Uday smiled. "Clever boy."

"With the newspapers, the limbs were patted dry—I got them six rolls of paper towels—and transferred onto dry newspapers about two or three pieces together, wrapped and put into plastic bags. The head … I went to the kitchen when I heard a commotion and, without looking in, I asked Big what was going on. Apparently, Small was holding the head in front of him, his fingers grasping the hair. He was talking to it! No idea what they were saying, but Big said he was scolding Small and demanding he wrap the head immediately. As soon as Small realised I knew what was going on, he did as Big told him to. The head was the last to be wrapped up and placed in the bin liners. They did a brilliant job of scrubbing the place down, even brushing the grouting between the wall tiles in the shower stall. I swear they left it cleaner than when they arrived."

"Let's hope that doesn't raise suspicions with Wilson, the agent. How messy was it anyway? There shouldn't have been too much blood splattering from a dead body, surely?"

"I don't think it splattered as much as it would have from a live body, but there was a little. Having kept the corpse cold for a few hours helped. It was mostly from sections of the body being chopped with some force. It was still bleeding, from what I saw of the rags and the paper towels used to clean it all up."

Uday turned to Ashwin and patted his shoulder. "Good job. It was a most undignified and crude death, befitting such a creature."

"I'm not finished, Dad—"

Uday shook his head and waved his finger in front of Ashwin. "No, enough. Really, I don't want to hear another word."

"This is the best part, Dad! I promise. It's good. You'll be pleased."

Uday rolled his eyes. "Okay. Go on."

"While those guys were packing various bits into bin liners, I put on latex gloves and gathered her clothes and handbag for dumping. Look what I found." Ashwin reached into his pocket and handed Uday an old iPhone. "I went through her messages. Everything's in Chinese. I'm sure there were conversations or calls with Tamara. Sayana might be able to help. Surely he would do that, at least?"

As Ashwin turned off the Ayer Rajah Expressway into Corporation Road, Uday looked out on both sides and asked, "Where are we?"

"Jurong. Not far from the bird park. Trust me, I know where I'm going."

"How did you know to come here?"

"I came here once with Angela to get meat. This company is a supplier to restaurants and sells the goods at a slight mark-up from wholesale prices. But it's a lot cheaper than the supermarket, so we save a lot, considering how much meat we eat and how often we entertain."

Ashwin turned into Fifth Chin Bee Road and slowed down to a crawl a few hundred metres before his destination. He did not see cameras anywhere. Most factories and warehouses still seemed to favour guard dogs or watchmen, sometimes both.

Uday breathed through his teeth and said, "I'm not sure this is a good idea, Ashwin. I cannot believe a place that stocks valuable food would not have a security camera."

"They probably have it inside, and all over as well. But out here? The gates are locked. Why would they monitor the road? I don't see any cameras around and they'd need more than these street lights to capture us throwing something in their bin."

Perumal said, "I think this place good, Sir. Can throw one bag. Big bin outside. I go now?"

"Yes. Put your hood up, cover as much of your face as possible and go quickly."

Through their closed doors and wound up windows, Uday and Ashwin heard the muted sound of a soft landing. Perumal dashed back into the car and announced that it was Babu's turn next.

Ashwin next drove to a residential estate in the north. "I picked one area each in the northern, southern, eastern and western parts of Singapore. Two industrial, two residential and one … you'll see."

"What do mean, 'you'll see'? No surprises, please, Ashwin. There is absolutely no room for error here."

"Next stop, Bukit Batok. Does it sound familiar?"

"Tell me, Ashwin."

"Their third rat infestation in as many years. It's been in the papers. I'm quite sure where we're going will have a lot more rats than humans at this hour. Foraging, I suppose. Just as well we used three layers of heavy-duty bags."

Ashwin made it sound like this was all fun and games. He had liked being the class jester and was punished often for his antics at school. He was extremely close to Lavinia and after what had happened, perhaps he now saw this as his mission. To get justice for Lavinia. Uday hoped his attitude was nothing more than his way of making light of a bad situation.

As Ashwin drove into the small carpark of Block 633 at Bukit Batok Central, two wide bins came into full view, lined up along a wall near the market. The place was deserted. Through the block of flats on his right, the clanging of woks and shrill voices shouting out orders cut through the carpark. It was almost 11pm. Must be hungry workers getting supper on their way home from working late.

Without waiting for Ashwin's prompt, Babu stepped out as soon as the car stopped. Whistling, he sauntered to the bin, lifted the cover with his index finger and chucked the bag in, and closed the bin quietly. He smiled and wobbled his head, the way many Indians do, to convey a positive sentiment, as he walked back towards the car.

Perumal and Babu chatted briefly in Tamil as Ashwin told everyone that he was now driving to Changi, near Singapore's easternmost tip. Uday tuned in to his favourite station, Hugs 94. Cringing at the deejay's fake American accent, he switched it to BBC.

"What was wrong with Hugs 94, Dad? I thought you liked it."

"Only the morning show. This evening deejay spoke like he was rolling pebbles in his mouth. I don't understand this obsession with American accents. The morning deejays speak perfectly, like Singaporeans—"

"Most people here don't speak English that well. But yes, I hate those fake accents. I use my iPod, got my Coldplay and Ed Sheeran plus lots more in acoustic, Brit pop, alternative rock … All without annoying deejays and commercials. Sometimes, I tune in to 938FM for traffic information and the news."

Uday realised that he had no idea what kind of music Ashwin liked. One day, he would ask to listen to some of Ashwin's music, to learn exactly what Britpop and alternative rock sounded like. That kind of music might make a nice change from his limited, yet eclectic, collection of CDs, which had an overly large number of Queen, Billy Joel, Genesis and Fleetwood Mac.

They headed towards Changi, with BBC broadcasting softly from the speakers. Uday was awed by the number of high-rise government housing blocks which lined both sides of the three expressways Ashwin took on their drive to Changi Point.

As they drove past the tree-lined Loyang Avenue, colonial low-rise buildings, with their wooden louvred and large balconies all lit with warm yellow light, were in stark contrast to the modern, box like units which sprouted to the sky in garish white fluorescence. This was a Singapore he had only ever read about but never seen. For such a small island, Uday was embarrassed by his limited knowledge of his adopted country. He had simply not bothered to discover an island which revealed a few gems if one only bothered to look.

They were barely a kilometre away from the end of the road where the shops, bars and restaurants were, when Ashwin saw the familiar blue light of a police car in his rear-view mirror.

"Pretend to be laughing and chatting, just in case they drive past us. Hey, Perumal, Babu, bend down as low as you can. Stay below the window."

"No space, sir."

Uday swung around to relieve them of the bags and placed them at his feet. The men then leaned across each other. Uday saw from his wing mirror that the police car maintained its speed and was unlikely to get past them.

Uday was puzzled. "Why do they have to hide?"

"Because I'm always being mistaken for a foreigner. A foreigner, possibly two, if they think you're not local either, and two migrant workers out here, at this time, might raise suspicions. The small one looks especially creepy and is capable of staring at the cops as they pass us, assuming they do. Let's not take any chances, Dad. There's a car park at the back of these buildings. I'm going to turn in there. We'll be fine, just police patrolling the area."

Perumal moaned. "Back pain. Can sit now, Sir?"

"No. Stay there till I say you can sit up."

Except for a few shuttered shops, the bars and restaurants

on both sides of Changi Village Road were overflowing with a motley group of people—young and old, of nearly every ethnic group in Singapore, some in office attire, while most were in shorts and t-shirts.

"It's past eleven o'clock on a week night. How can people eat so late? Don't they have to sleep?"

"Wednesday. Ladies Night at the bars. Discounted drinks for women. It's an island-wide thing. Besides, I think most of them live around here and probably work at Changi Business Park, which is ten minutes away, on the other side of Changi Airport."

"Aren't we supposed to stick to quiet places?"

"Yes, but this is an exception. Lots and lots of food waste bins here, and no cameras, no parking gantries."

Ashwin turned into the carpark of Block 5, Changi Village Road. "You and Babu can sit up now, Perumal. Whose turn is it?"

Perumal reached towards Uday's side and asked for a bag. Uday was alarmed to find only two bags. "We started with five bags, and now we only have two. One's missing!"

Perumal replied, "Sorry sir, I have one here, at my feet. This is very bad bag."

Ashwin whispered to Uday, "The head. Don't worry, Dad, I've only had you handle the ones with chopped limbs and her stuff."

Ashwin stopped the car somewhere near the middle of the car park, facing the backs of the bars and restaurants. There were at least ten bins in total, all lined up against the wall of their respective food and beverage establishments.

Uday noticed stray cats everywhere, especially near the bins, and under the trees at the sides. "There must be at least twenty stray cats here. They seem to be waiting to scrounge in the bins. You think this is safe?"

"Absolutely. Those bins are the newer designs, introduced a year ago to prevent cats and rats from climbing on to them and lifting the covers. Those cats are just waiting to get lucky. I'm sure the staff in these places feed them with scraps. I've seen it often at Holland Village."

"How sweet of them," said Uday, staring at the bins.

Perumal asked, "Which bin, sir?"

Ashwin pointed to the one two doors away from where he was parked. "That one. The satay shop. Similar kind of food waste."

Uday felt peckish when he smelt barbecued meat. The sign read, "Come here for Best Satay in Singapore!" Uday was tempted. "Do you think we should take a break? Maybe get some satay? Fancy some?"

Ashwin checked the clock on the dashboard and glanced towards the open door of the restaurant's kitchen. "It's late, Dad. And looking at how busy the kitchen is, it could be a long wait, but if you insist, go ahead."

Uday stared at the signboard as he watched Perumal ambling towards the car with his hands in his pocket. "No, best not to. Not worth the risk in case my order leaves a trail we cannot hide."

Ashwin started the engine as soon as Perumal shut the door. "Get ready, people. We're off to look for a boat."

"You never said anything about a boat. We agreed that one bag will be sunk in the river near the stadium. A boat involves a witness. What's wrong with you, Ashwin?"

"The sea is safer than the river, Dad. The boatman doesn't care. He'll probably just assume I'm throwing away the cremated remains of a close relative. Hindus have specific times for these things so it's not like this hour would raise any suspicion."

"Ashes? In a bin liner? Which will probably float back up.

He'll believe you, you think? Let's just get away for here. I think sleep deprivation is making you reckless."

"Dad, I know this area really well. Spent nearly all my army years around here. You're right about the boatman. But that bag still needs to be sunk and it's better for us to dump it around here, rather than at the Kallang River."

Ashwin drove out of the carpark and turned right into Changi Point Road. At the traffic lights he turned left into Telok Paku Road. As he approached a curve fifty metres ahead, Ashwin slowed down and checked for traffic, before stopping at a bridge. When they were both sure there weren't any cars around, Ashwin asked Perumal to take the bag he had, which was also the smallest but heaviest bag, and throw it in the river. The smell of diesel and stale seaweed filled the car as soon as Perumal opened the door. Within seconds, they heard a hard splash, courtesy of the large river stones Ashwin had salvaged from the top of his potted plants. Uday and Ashwin looked at each other briefly, satisfied that the head of a monster, along with her severed hands and feet, had made its way through filthy water and hit the muddy bed of Sungei Changi, destined to rot away with the currents.

Uday felt a sea burial, even if only for body parts, was too kind for what Sharon had done to Lavinia. Rubbish dumps were far more appropriate.

Perumal got back in and slammed the car door shut as Babu chided him for taking his turn. Perumal ignored him and simply said to Ashwin, "Next one for Babu, sir. Last stop."

Ashwin yawned as he turned on the radio. "Yes, one last stop. We've covered the west, north and east, two stops in the east. We're now south-bound to dump her things."

As they made a U-turn on Telok Paku Road, heading back towards Loyang Avenue, Ashwin saw a rubbish bin outside the

Hindu temple on the corner, next to the traffic lights. "Look, Dad! A huge rubbish bin outside a little temple. I wonder why. Maybe they have feasts here on auspicious occasions." Ashwin stopped outside the temple, and again, checked to see if there were any cars or people around.

"A temple. We kill a woman, butcher her body and use a temple's precincts to get rid of the evidence. Even as an atheist, I feel there's something not quite right about that." Uday handed back the last bin bag which he had earlier taken from the two men. "I don't like the idea of my feet kicking against it every now and then, even if it's just her things."

Ashwin drove away from the temple. "You're right. Not a good idea anyway, to have three bags within a kilometre of each other. I was getting lazy."

"And complacent." Uday yawned. "I'm ready to call it quits." Uday saw the signs for the airport. "The airport must be no more than ten minutes away. Why can't we drive them straight there? We'll drop the last bag off ourselves somewhere near home, which is close enough to the south."

"Who's being complacent now? The airport is full of cameras! We can't put ourselves in places where we could be filmed with them. Added precaution. Just taking your advice, Dad. Let's just drop them off near Serangoon Road, where they can get a cab. They'll just look like two men out of over a hundred all over Singapore, on any given night, who head for the airport to catch the 3am flight to Chennai."

As they neared Serangoon Road, Uday retrieved a large manila envelope from under his seat. He opened it and checked that the eight stacks of hundred-dollar notes were intact.

They spoke in Hindi. "Five thousand in a stack. Forty thousand, twenty each. That's what you promised them, right?"

"Yes, but that was to kill the bastard as well. I ended up being the murderer. We should give them half." Ashwin turned around to speak to Perumal and Babu, but Uday cut him off.

"How much each were you promised?"

Perumal answered. "Twenty."

"But you didn't do the hardest part. You should get less. Ten."

"Fifteen."

Babu wanted to know what they were discussing. Perumal told him. Babu chimed in, "Feeteen!"

Uday waved his hand. The two men had taken on the worst task—chopping, cooking and packing the parts, especially the head. That alone was worth a tidy sum.

"Fine, have your fifteen each." Ashwin slowed down and stopped outside the shops along Serangoon Road, shutters down and litter lining the corridor and pavements. He turned around and spoke to Perumal. "You know you don't deserve that much but that's what you'll get. But if you so much as say a word about this, trust me, I will find men to hunt you down and kill you. Don't mess with me."

"Sir, I won't talk. Babu also. We want to forget Singapore. Very bad place. Your money will give us new life. Good life. Maybe after few months, we go to Qatar. Build stadium for World Cup."

"Qatar? Much worse than Singapore, we've heard."

"Like lottery, sir. For some people, Singapore good. For some people, Qatar good. Maybe for Babu and me, Qatar good. We try."

Uday wished them luck as Ashwin handed over the money and their passports. "You're done—"

"No, they're not. Just one more, Dad. Let them finish it. I'll drive to Holland Village. I know the perfect spot."

"Near Dr Dubash's?"

"Yes. There's a market next to his block." Ashwin turned to Perumal. "Where's the plastic bag, Perumal?"

"Next to my feet, sir. I throw?"

"Leave that to me. It won't be a problem. You can catch a taxi from here. Grab your bags and go. Good luck."

"Sir, you please go Syed Alwi Road. More easy to find taxi and many place to throw bag. Now quiet. Very safe, sir."

Ashwin did as Perumal asked, stopping at the junction of Lembu Road. While Babu removed the luggage from the boot, Perumal ran to a bin near an alley and hurled the last bag in.

Ashwin thanked the men and drove off.

By 1am on Thursday, Sharon Lin had been strangled, dismembered, cooked, her body parts thrown into the sea and into four rubbish bins all across Singapore.

24

Early Hours, Thursday

Uday and Ashwin sat in the rented car in the basement parking lot of their condominium.

"You okay, Dad?"

Uday shook his head slowly and leant back. "Up until a few days ago, we were decent people. Today we're no different from hardcore criminals."

"I wouldn't put it quite like that, Dad. But yes, we committed a crime. I killed her. Maybe someday, I'll regret it. When Lavinia is well and living a happy, healthy life years from now, I might think it wasn't necessary to kill that devil. Right now, though, I feel nothing but relief to know she is out of our lives."

"We won't be entirely safe until we deal with that other, bigger, problem."

"I know, but right now, Dad, we both need some sleep. I really want to see Lavinia first thing in the morning."

Uday thought of the crucifix above Lavinia's bed. "There is something so unjust, so cruel, about the good Catholic girl, the one who symbolises purity and goodness more than anyone in our family, to be so viciously attacked and to be fighting for her life. I'm glad her new-found religion gave her the comfort I didn't even know she was seeking, but right now, I am angry with her god for not protecting her enough, for failing her in her time of need."

Ashwin snorted. "She must've prayed for her life as she begged for mercy. Where was divine intervention when she needed it? I'll always be a devout atheist, Dad. Especially after this." Ashwin yawned and let out a soft whoop. "As I'm sure you can tell, I am dead exhausted."

"Me, too. But I'd like to see Sayana and ask for his help with those phone messages. I'm sure they're all there, messages between mother and daughter. And the two men who … who …" Uday bit his knuckles and faced the window.

"We know what they did, Dad. No need to torment yourself by spelling it out. Let's sleep on it. See you later in the morning." Ashwin handed the keys to Uday. "Don't forget to ask Wati to wash the car, and to give the interior a proper wipe down. Remind her to use gloves! Don't forget another wipe down when you leave it at the car park. Wipe the key with your handkerchief before putting it in a re-sealable bag or pouch. Also—"

"I know what I need to do, Ashwin. Trust me. Go get some sleep."

"We're all tired and it's easy to forget certain details."

"Yes … yes, my son. I didn't pay eight hundred dollars in cash just to rent this toy car, for which Grab drivers pay a mere eighty a day. Paying ten times more was the cost of covering our tracks with no questions asked."

Uday checked his phone. Eleven missed calls from Tamara. She had probably driven herself insane wondering what was going on. Uday smiled, left his phone on silent mode, placed it on the charger and went to bed.

The room was pitch dark when Uday sat upright, jolted by a dream. Lavinia had sat by his bed and asked him where he had been. She told him about her first day as an intern at the migrant workers' welfare centre. There were two men who had dropped by in the early afternoon and given Lavinia five thousand dollars. A donation, they said, to help the hundreds of workers abused and injured with nowhere to go, while they waited for justice from the Ministry of Manpower. Justice which is either slow or non-existent because employers game the system. Lavinia laughed as she described them—Obelix and Asterix. Uday was about to laugh along with her when he woke up.

The clock said 8.04. Uday jumped out of bed and drew open the blackout curtains. He turned away from the glare. It was a hot and sunny morning. He checked his phone again. Another six missed calls and eight messages from Tamara.

Uday called Tamara. She answered before he even heard the ring tone.

"Uday! I've been trying to reach you since yesterday afternoon! Where were you?" Tamara was livid, her voice shaking, her tone cold.

Uday used his business voice, the one he reserved for potential partners who played hardball, yet whose partnership he coveted. He smiled as he spoke with a light touch, a musical lilt. "Tamara! I'm very well, thank you. And how are you?"

"Where were you? Why didn't you answer your phone? Hundred times I tried to call you." Uday could imagine her sulking while admiring yet another fresh manicure.

"Darling, I've been so busy—"

"Too busy for me?" She had suddenly switched to that coy younger woman he had pursued some years ago. Her voice was so sweet, he could taste the cloying stickiness in his mouth. It sickened him.

Uday laughed. "No, of course not, my darling. It's just that so much has happened. I've been meaning to call you but was waiting to make sure everything was alright—"

"What happened? So, is Lavi going to be alright? It must be so hard for you." Tamara was sounding quite the actress. It made it easier for Uday to string her along. Fun, even.

"I have excellent news for you. Lavi made a miraculous recovery yesterday. Opened her eyes on her own, recognised people, said a few words. It was magic. Only Angela was there at the time, but she called all of us and we rushed to the hospital to witness it ourselves. The doctor could only describe it as a miracle. Said he'd never seen anything like it in all his years in medicine. We're all thrilled! Of course, it'll be some time before she comes home, but for now, it looks like in time, Lavi will be her beautiful, happy self again."

There was a pause. Uday wondered if Tamara had heard everything he said. Sometimes, intermittent breaks in calls to China were to be expected.

"Hello? Tamara, are you there?"

"Yes, yes, Uday, I'm here. Sorry, I was a little distracted."

"With what?"

"Oh, nothing. Just … just looking for my … earrings." She was a terrible liar.

"Uday, I'm a bit worried. I haven't heard from Sharon in a few days. I tried calling many times but there's no answer. Can you please check on her?"

"But you hardly ever speak to her. You're always saying she never calls and yet on those rare occasions when she calls, you yell at her. And you wonder why she doesn't call. When was the last time you spoke to her, or even bothered to see her?"

"I saw her two weeks ago but last spoke to her on Sunday morning."

Uday nodded and smiled. Tamara was not as bright as he'd thought. "That's barely four days ago. I'm sure she'll call you next week. Or maybe you should just come back soon and pay her a visit. Maybe you're right, you should fly out tonight. Not for me, but for Sharon."

"For you especially, Uday." That voice again. Uday shuddered. "You'll send the car?"

Why not, thought Uday. It would be her last ride in his newly serviced BMW 750Li. "Yes, of course."

Uday had a quick shower, called the office for updates, asked for his afternoon meeting to be cancelled and promised to be in by 4pm.

Lavinia looked the same as when he had last seen her nearly twenty-four hours ago. A nurse walked in to check her vitals. Uday asked to see the doctor as he sank into the armchair next to her bed.

A young man who looked like a medical student knocked as he entered the room. Uday stood up and walked towards him. Extending his hand, the young man said, "Hello, I'm Doctor Low, Miss Aurora's neurologist. You must be her father?" Uday made no effort to hide his consternation. "Oh, I'm thirty-six, Mr Aurora. I get this a lot, especially from parents. Your daughter is in good hands, I assure you."

Uday shook the doctor's hand. "Yes, I'm her father. Why are you here? What happened to her other doctor, Professor Goh?"

"I'm so sorry, Mr Aurora, but Professor Goh had to take emergency leave. He flew to Kuala Lumpur last night to visit his father, who is very ill."

Uday felt bad for lashing out at the young doctor. "How is she, Doctor Low?"

Dr Low took a deep breath. "It's hard to say. Did Professor

Goh give you an update yesterday?"

"Only to say that there was no improvement and that she was being closely monitored. Is there anything else you can tell me?

"Based on her response in the first twenty-four hours of severe brain injury, statistics—"

"Statistics? And what? Lies? No, don't give me statistics. My child is not a number. Tell me what you think her chances are, given your assurance that she is in good hands."

"Mr Aurora, I can only hazard a guess, given the information I have now. Miss Lavinia has not opened her eyes. She has not made a sound, which means she has not shown signs of speech. She withdraws from painful stimuli—"

"Painful stimuli? You are deliberately inflicting pain on my daughter?"

"Oh no, nothing like that, Mr Aurora. It's a technique to assess a patient's level of consciousness, especially as with Miss Lavinia. Professor Goh went through the same motions when Miss Lavinia was first admitted. We first performed a trapezium squeeze test near her shoulder, away from the broken area. Miss Lavinia grimaced. We then pinched the sides of her finger, but there was no response. Based on a scale we use, the Glasgow Coma Scale, Miss Lavinia's score is four out of fifteen, which means she has suffered severe brain injury—"

"We already knew that her injuries were severe, but what are her chances of recovery? Is she brain dead?"

Dr Low hesitated. "I don't know for sure, Mr Aurora. It's hard to make a prognosis until at least two weeks later. All I can tell you now is that her brain injury is irreversible, and that she is breathing via a ventilator."

Uday gazed at Lavinia and stroked her hair. "I really hate statistics, but what are her chances, Doctor? Please tell me honestly." The numbers would have a bearing on what he would decide to do with Tamara.

Dr Low took a deep breath. "If Miss Lavinia does not emerge from her coma within a month, it means that when she does emerge, she will most likely be severely disabled. Based on Miss Lavinia's score of four on the scale, she falls into the category where almost ninety percent of such patients either die soon after or remain in a vegetative state. Then again, that means about ten percent do recover, so—"

"Say if she's one of the ten percent—will she be able to practice law? Play Scrabble, or tennis?"

Dr Low glanced at Lavinia. "We can only wait and see, Mr Aurora."

Uday nodded as he turned to Lavinia and continued gazing at her, stroking her forehead with the back of his finger. The wounds on both sides of her face were still bandaged, with pus from the wound on her right side oozing and staining the gauze just beneath the surface. "My beautiful child. I won't let anyone hurt you ever again. You will be safe. I promise."

25

Later That Day

"Mama, come." I keep hoping for a miracle, hoping to hear her whisper those words. She had uttered them regularly, ever since that day, years ago, in hospital, when I was on my way out, when Uday and the boys had gathered to say their goodbyes. Lavinia was ten years old, but she cried like when she was a toddler and couldn't find her blanket. She leant towards me, supported by her little elbows, and kissed me. With what little strength I had left in my decaying body, I turned to face her, before looking at Uday and the boys. I whispered, "Just say, Mama, come. I will be there. You won't see me, nor hear me, but I'll be there. Okay?"

Lavinia had smiled through her tears and nodded. "Mama, come."

Hours later, I left.

That night, the whole family sat at home, calling friends and relatives. The cremation was scheduled for noon the next day, followed by a reception at home. Uday had chuckled when months before, I had joked about how atheists make weddings and funerals so much easier by eliminating the religious component. Yes, he had said, especially for Indians—we can simply focus on the party.

It was my idea to have a party. We'd been to a few funerals

where it really felt like more than one person had died. We had mourned, separately and together, the loss of loved ones in years past, but for my own departure, I wanted a celebration. Something small, with my dearest friends, a multi-national group of women—neighbours, school mothers, tennis partners, friends of friends—all of whom had welcomed me when we first arrived in Singapore. They were a big part of my charmed life in my adopted home. I insisted on picking the caterer—Indian food, real and good, none of that Indian-Chinese pretend food Uday used to love until we moved to Singapore. The music was not to Uday's taste, but it was on my personal top of the pops list—Kate Bush, The Who, The Pretenders, George Michael— and lots of champagne.

I wanted another little party in London, for my friends from school and university. Similar to the Singapore party—a few friends, good food, good music and drinks, more likely to be gin and vodka rather than champagne. After that, Uday, the children, my parents and my siblings would drive to the Scottish West Highlands and take the Jacobite Steam Train. It was where Uday and I had spent many term breaks while we were at Edinburgh University. We loved the raw, rugged beauty of the Highlands. The people were always warm and kind towards us.

One summer, after our first year, we had taken the West Highland train from Fort William to Mallaig. The woman at the B&B at Fort William had urged us to take the ride just for the Glenfinnan viaduct crossing. It was the most spectacular train ride I had been on, and I had been on many, having spent all my life in England. On the way back, just as we were crossing the viaduct, I had said to Uday, when I die, I'd like my ashes scattered out of the window at this spot. He had laughed and said he would be too old, or possibly dead, by then, and we'd have to leave that to the children.

That's when he said he didn't care how many children we had, as long as we had a daughter. Girls can be anything boys want to be and still be girls, loving and caring towards their parents. He was convinced all daughters would be like his sisters—one an engineer and the other a photographer, both extremely filial—and me. We were lucky with Lavinia.

I had forgotten about having my ashes scattered out of a train on the Glenfinnan viaduct. Uday reminded me. When he first discussed the plans with the children, Lavinia had bawled, saying a party was a happy thing but Mama's death was a sad thing, and everyone had to be sad. Everyone had to cry every day and wear black for the rest of their lives.

It took a while for Ashwin and Sayana to explain that Mama was so special and happy and enjoyed life so much that she had asked for a party. Everyone had to be happy and wear colourful clothes and celebrate her life. Lavinia seemed puzzled, and though still heartbroken, agreed to go along with the rest of the family in fulfilling my wishes.

Lavinia's mood shifted the moment she was told about Scotland.

"We're going on Hogwart's Express?" Ashwin and Sayana had laughed at how quickly she had smiled, her eyes lighting up, as they had done every time she stood in front of her cake—invariably in the form of a Disney princess—which was wheeled towards her at her birthday parties.

"Better than that!"

"Hogwart's Express is the best train!"

"The Royal Scotsman is even better. Super luxurious, with yummy food, and it's really comfortable. Trains aren't always comfortable, or even clean, you know."

"Super expensive, too!" Sayana rubbed his thumb against his

bent forefinger to signal the counting of money.

"We'll cross that special bridge, the same one we always see in Harry Potter films. That's when we'll say a final bye-bye to Mama."

"Why do we have to say that? Mama is still here. She's dead, but not really. I talk to her all the time. She doesn't always talk back. Only sometimes. But she always listens."

Ashwin looked at Sayana and turned back to Lavinia. "What do you mean, Lavi?"

"I told you! She's here." Lavinia pointed to the floor near the cupboard where I was sitting. The boys turned to look.

"I don't see Mama."

"Nor do I."

In the early weeks, I had spoken to the boys, shown myself to them, but they never heard me, nor saw me. It was the same with Uday, though sometimes I think he felt my presence.

"I see Mama. And I'm not saying bye-bye to Mama."

The boys hugged Lavinia and promised her that Mama would be happy with their plans.

"Mama will be at the party," said Lavinia as she faced my direction and smiled at me.

It was a delightful event. Most of the people I really liked were there. A few were travelling. Lavinia wore her long, blue Cinderella dress and asked Maribel to put her hair up, exactly like Cinderella at the ball. As no one could find a blonde wig for such a small head, Maribel used golden sparkly spray instead. Lavinia told me that night that she felt like a fairy tale princess, like Cinderella herself.

I stroke her arm and tell her, *You are a fairy tale princess and always will be.* I've been saying that several times a day since we arrived at this hospital room.

Like Sleeping Beauty, I want to believe my fairy tale princess will wake up.

26

Tamara was getting dressed for dinner when Uday arrived home from the hospital. She sashayed towards him and threw her arms around his neck.

"Did you miss me, Uday?"

"Of course!" Uday was glad Tamara couldn't see his face. "You're all dressed up. Going out?"

"I thought we could go out for dinner. I feel restless. I've asked Pin Hui and John to join us."

Uday threw his shoulders back and groaned. "Why did you not think to ask me? They are the most boring people I know. I've said that before! She doesn't say a word and all he ever talks about is himself. I have no idea why you think I'd want to spend an evening with them. We've never done that. Cancel it."

"Exactly why I arranged it. Because we've never done this before and I thought you liked them. They've been asking us to dinner for months but you're always busy. What am I supposed to say to them?"

"I don't know. You got us into this, you get us out of it. We're having dinner at home. We've got a special meal arranged." Uday held her chin and smiled as he spoke. "Just for you. Now, don't be so grumpy, my darling." Uday walked towards the dresser, removing his cufflinks. "Call your friend. Cancel the dinner."

Tamara called her friend. Her voice soft and weary, she said, "So sorry, we can't make it. I feel quite sick … Yes, that, too. Tired from the flight … Yes, we'll arrange something soon … yes, within the next few weeks. I'll check Uday's schedule and get back to you."

By 8pm, the whole family had gathered at the table for a feast.

Instead of Tamara sitting by his side as she usually did, Uday asked her to sit at the other end of the table, directly opposite him. "So I can spend the evening looking at you. I've missed you." Uday felt nauseous as he spoke.

Ashwin sat on his left, while Angela sat on his right. Sayana scowled as he took his seat between Tamara and Angela, while Priyanka sat between Tamara and Ashwin. Sayana, without making any effort to be subtle, dragged his chair closer to Angela. Uday was about to admonish Sayana for being ungracious when he noticed a momentary smirk on Tamara's pink-tinged lips, followed soon after by what must have been a curse in Chinese.

"It's a shame Lavi can't join us." Ashwin raised his glass. "May our beautiful sister come home soon!" Uday rose with the rest of the family. Tamara remained seated until Priyanka jabbed her arm. While everyone raised their glasses, no one except Tamara could pretend to be joyous. It was the most mournful toast Uday had participated in, with Tamara masterfully disguising her rage with feigned sorrow.

The first course was spiced pea soup with mint, drizzled with yogurt. The only sound was the spoons dragging against the soup plates, seemingly everyone's at the same time. Uday, never good at making small talk, broke the silence. "How was your trip, Tamara? Your parents alright?"

"They are fine—"

"Fine? I thought your mother was dying," said Priyanka, with genuine surprise.

"Very sick, yes, but not dying. Now she is much better and is home."

"Quite a recovery, then, for an old woman," said Priyanka.

Tamara ignored Priyanka as she smiled at Uday. "My parents send their regards. They want to come for the wedding, but Mother might not be well enough to travel, and Father won't go anywhere without her. They asked if we could fly to Shanghai for the tea ceremony. For them, we won't be considered married until we go through that ritual."

Both Ashwin and Sayana peered over their soup towards Uday, who cleared his throat as he spoke. "Yes, of course. We must do that."

Once the soup plates were cleared, Wati and Conchita brought out the main courses. With each serving dish placed on the table, they announced what they had spent the day preparing: cauliflower with turmeric and cumin; cod, pan seared and lightly cooked in a spicy tomato sauce; black *dal* with cream; cucumber and tomato salad; mushroom pilaf, and *kofta* curry.

"The *piece de resistance*," said Uday, as he raised his water glass and beamed. As instructed by Ashwin earlier that evening, Wati placed the bowl of *kofta* curry between Tamara and Priyanka, who, like everyone else except Tamara, had earlier been told not to eat any of it until cued to do so. "The menu was planned by Angela and Pri."

While everyone helped themselves to the various dishes and passed the bowls around, Tamara heaped spoonfuls of the *kofta* curry onto her plate before adding the other items.

"Mmmm. This is delicious! My favourite Indian dish." Tamara picked up the bowl and gestured to Sayana to pass it to

Uday. "You must have some, Uday! One bite and you'll be non-vegetarian again."

"Thank you, Tamara, but I like being vegetarian. I'll help myself later. Go ahead, take as much as you want," Uday said, as Sayana placed the serving bowl right in front of Tamara, suppressing his characteristic snigger as he did so.

After making sure Tamara was looking in his direction, Ashwin winked at Uday, who nodded. "Tamara, I heard you were having trouble contacting Sharon. Did you manage to reach her when you got back?"

Tamara sighed. "No. I am so worried. I asked Aaron—"

Uday dropped his fork on to his plate. "Aaron is back? When? He's not here, in this flat, is he?"

"I called to tell him I was coming back today, a few days earlier. He arrived this afternoon. Maybe he's out now."

Uday's sons and their wives exchanged glances. Perhaps Lavinia was right—perhaps there *was* something going on between Tamara and Aaron.

Uday pursed his lips. "What did you ask Aaron to do?"

Tamara's expression changed. She twirled the corner of her napkin as she stared at her plate and spoke in a soft voice. "I asked him to go over to Sharon's flat. It seems she left on Wednesday morning to work as a private chef—"

"I thought she worked in a restaurant," said Sayana.

"She does but on Mondays, when the restaurant is closed, she freelances as a private chef. She has her regulars who call her for dinner parties—"

Priyanka interrupted. "On a Monday evening?"

"Why not? We Chinese like to eat early. Finish early."

Uday stared straight at Tamara. "But Wednesday isn't her day off. Where do you think Sharon is?"

Tamara placed her napkin by her side and leant against the ornate dining chair. Rubbing the gilt, cushioned arm, she stared at the contents of her plate and said, "I don't know. Sometimes she gets requests on other days and her clients pay her a lot more. She didn't say anything to her friend except that her client was Indonesian, was paying her a lot of money and that she would be picked up at a bus stop. I am afraid for her."

"Afraid? More than worried? Why would you be afraid? Singapore's so safe!" Ashwin turned away and winked at Sayana, who sulked. "Has she done something wrong? Got mixed up with some bad company?"

Tamara shook her head, her curls dancing across her shoulders. "She's a good girl. But many people here don't like people from China, so maybe something happened to her."

Ashwin chuckled. "Maybe some people aren't pleased about the wave of workers from China, but that's hardly a reason to harm someone. Maybe Sharon isn't as good as you think? Maybe she is nothing but a vile little shit—"

Tamara stood up and threw her napkin at Ashwin. "Don't you dare call my daughter that!"

Ashwin laughed again. "Your daughter? Didn't you think it was odd that we knew about this daughter only two days ago? Because Dad mentioned it to us when you got worried? Look at you, former Miss Shandong—"

"Miss Shanghai! Very prestigious! I was Miss Shanghai, winner of a contest with China's most beautiful women. Shandong is a province; the women there are peasants."

Tamara curled her lips and looked away, trying to catch her reflection in the mirror above the sideboard.

Ashwin and Sayana shook their heads and smiled at each other. "She's quite amazing. Her daughter could be dead and she's all, oooooh, look at me, I'm Miss Shanghai! I'm not a peasant." Ashwin mocked Tamara by putting on a high-pitched voice and making feminine gestures with his hands.

Tamara sprang from her chair. "How dare you! What is wrong with you? Uday, tell them to stop being so disrespectful!"

Uday laughed. "Tamara, sit down." Tamara glared at Uday. With her hands on her hips, her eyes narrowed to mere slits, she said, "No. Try and make me."

Ashwin laughed. "Ohhhhh, Tamara Wang. You don't want Dad to do that. I'd sit down if I were you. Right now."

Tamara slunk slowly into her seat. Uday lowered his voice. "First, tell me what happened to Lavinia."

"Lavinia? How would I know? You said she was attacked and she's getting better."

"You know that's not true. She's supposed to be dead, isn't she?"

"How would I know?"

"That's your response? I thought you might ask, pretending to gasp at first, why would she be dead? Cue a few more gasps."

"Okay then, why would she be dead?"

"Too little, too late. I heard from a very reliable source that you ordered the rape and murder—"

"What?"

"You heard me. You ordered the rape and murder of Lavinia."

"So you lied to me. Lavinia is actually dead?"

Ashwin laughed and thumped the table. "You order my sister's killing and you're upset that my father lied to you about what really happened? You really are a psychopath. No. Lavinia is not dead. So sorry to disappoint you. By the way, did you like the *koftas*? As delicious as you exclaimed upon the first bite?"

Tamara frowned. "Yes, I liked them. Stop changing the subject. If Lavinia is alive, then where is my daughter?"

Uday got up, picked up the bowl which had been sitting in front of Tamara, and placed it right under her nose. "Here she is. Made from her skinny thighs. You were too busy to notice that none of us touched this."

Tamara gagged and tried to push the bowl out of Uday's hands before he handed it to Sayana. She dashed to the powder room but was unable to make it in time.

"Oh yuck, it's on the floor! Poor Conchita will have to clean up because Miss Shanghai is unlikely to," said Angela with an excessive melodic lilt.

"Ashwin, I think you should call the cops."

"What am I supposed to say?"

Uday rolled his eyes. "I'll call them."

Soon after, Sayana and Priyanka answered the door bell and led four policemen to the dining area.

Tamara ran towards the policeman standing closest to the dining table and, sobbing as she pointed towards Uday, begged, "Arrest him! He killed my daughter. And then, then he …"

The oldest of the four, a policeman with grey hair and a stocky frame, asked her to sit down. He introduced himself as Inspector Lim.

"No! How can I sit down?" Switching to Chinese, Tamara rattled away in a shrill voice.

Sayana translated her version for the rest of the family. "She said you cooked her daughter. Hamburger curry. She swears she is innocent. She was in Shanghai. Uday is evil. He beats her often. She asked them to please arrest him and rescue her."

Priyanka smiled as she helped herself to two pieces of kofta and spooned another two onto Angela's plate.

The younger policeman, whose nametag read Ronald Teo and who was a constable according to Ashwin, told Tamara to be quiet. The other policeman, whose name was Ridzwan, repeated Constable Teo's command. Ashwin identified him as a Sergeant. Ashwin whispered to Uday, "People here aren't very good at introductions."

Uday raised his eyebrows. "So I see."

The fourth policeman introduced himself as Assistant Superintendent Belmont Lee.

Ashwin leant towards his father, "Unless they have a fancy title or name. In this case, both."

"Shush," Uday said as he waved Ashwin away, smiling as he remembered the time one of his colleagues had asked him to review the resume of a young hotel school graduate who called himself Ritz Chan.

The Assistant Superintendent—"Call me ASP Lee"—thrust his chest out slightly, scanned the room and glanced at everyone around the table. He walked towards Uday, asking, "Mr Aurora, you called us about an attempted murder. Could you please explain?"

Pointing towards Ashwin, Uday said, "Sorry, I didn't mean to mislead you. Not here but somewhere else. An on-going case in your files. My son has all the evidence. We managed to get Tamara's daughter's phone from her friend."

"Please start from the beginning, sir."

Uday narrated the events of Sunday night up until the time he had given the police his statement at the hospital. "All this information should be in your files."

Tamara jumped out of her seat and screamed, "How can you be sure it was my Sharon who tried to kill Lavi? But we are all sure you killed my daughter! You admitted it yourself. She's in … in … there!" Tamara pointed to the bowl as she wailed. "You people are worse than animals. Look at you! You are even eating her! Is she delicious? Monsters! Animals!" Turning to Sergeant Ridzwan, who was standing next to her, Tamara begged through tears, which messed up her make-up, "Please arrest him. He did such a bad thing to my beloved child. Oh, my poor child. How she must have suffered!"

Sergeant Ridzwan gently sat her down while warning her to be quiet.

ASP Lee turned towards Tamara and repeated Sergeant Ridzwan's warning in Mandarin. Addressing Uday and the rest of the family, he said, "There is still nothing that pins Ms Tamara to your daughter's alleged attempted murder."

Sayana frowned as he spoke. "There's nothing alleged about it. She did it. And she didn't just attack her, she tried to kill her! Please check your police report. It's all there. And if that's not enough, check these phones." Pointing at Tamara, Sayana said, "She, allegedly, is the loving mother. Go through that phone to see if this loving mother had any communication with her daughter during her first two months here and after that, for the three weeks after her return, until days before she left for China. Allegedly loving mother who is now distraught about her missing daughter."

ASP Lee breathed deeply and placed his notebook and pen on the table. He scrolled through the messages on Sharon's phone. "It's all in Chinese. I'll need to ask Constable Teo to translate all the messages." Handing Sharon's phone to the young policemen, ASP Lee said, "Get Ms Tamara's phone and go through the messages, especially between Ms Tamara and her daughter. Give me an update in ten minutes."

Tamara tried to run towards the bedroom, but was restrained by Sergeant Ridzwan, who accompanied her and Ashwin to the bedroom, where he saw her bag on the bed. Uday watched through the hallway as Tamara tried to free herself and lunge for the bag, but Sergeant Ridzwan managed to retrieve the phone and hand it to Constable Teo.

Constable Teo interrupted with a whisper. "Sir, the woman keeps insisting her daughter is in the meatball curry—"

"She has quite an imagination! Look at my sons and their wives still eating them. It's just a combination of minced beef, minced pork and a little bacon. Help yourself."

ASP Lee raised his hand. "Thank you, sir. We'll need to take some samples for testing."

Ashwin exclaimed, "You're kidding! You must be! You might want to believe we're cannibals, but you can't possibly imagine my pregnant wife would eat a human being!"

"Sir, please allow us to do what we need to do."

Uday waved towards the bowl, with all of three pieces of *kofta* left, drenched in gravy. "I understand. Please, help yourself. We only said that to taunt her. While my daughter barely clings to signs of life because of what *she* did to her, she is worried about her daughter, who we believe carried out the attack on her instructions."

ASP Lee pulled his chair away from the table and turned it around to face Uday. "Mr Aurora, up until the night your daughter was hospitalised, you had a suspect who was in Mumbai, correct? At what point did you realise Ms Tamara and her daughter were involved?"

"When we received her daughter's phone in the mailbox on Wednesday evening. There was no stamp or anything, so it must have been delivered by someone. The security guards could not identify who it was—"

"Aren't they supposed to have a record of who enters and leaves the condominium? Especially at a luxury condo like this?"

"I think they are but clearly they didn't bother, and I can only assume that usually they don't check."

"Tell me more about the phone."

"My son, Sayana," Uday nodded in Sayana's direction and continued, "is fluent in Chinese and translated the messages from the past week. A lot of words were in code—for example, tandoori meat, which, in the context, seemed to mean Lavinia. We were astounded.

"I refused to believe that this woman, this seductress I was going to marry, was behind my daughter being so viciously attacked and left in a coma. I tried to find out more about Sharon, to confront her, you know, to face the devil, before handing her over to the police. We called everyone in her contacts who had a local number. There weren't many, at the most twenty. Most said they hadn't heard from her in a long time. Some claimed they didn't know her. A few people asked a lot of questions and hung up. I knew I had to lure the culprit—"

"Culprit! Culprit! That's all you can say! I was in Shanghai. I had nothing to do with whatever happened to that daughter of yours—"

Sergeant Ridzwan patted Tamara's shoulder, "Madam, please ..."

Uday sighed, "That daughter of mine, who lies in hospital, her chances of survival diminishing by the day ... As I was saying, I could no longer pretend that all was well, and asked Tamara to return a week earlier. She was ready to fly out anyway because she hadn't heard from her daughter and was probably wondering how Lavinia was still alive—"

Tamara pushed her plate and cutlery off the table, sending them crashing onto the marble floor. In a voice hoarse from screaming, she spat out, "Ya! I wish she were dead! It's true! She hates me! Trying to turn you against me! But doesn't mean I did it, okay!"

Constable Teo returned with a phone in each hand and bent to whisper to ASP Lee, who frowned as he listened. Pursing his lips and frowning, he turned to Uday and asked, "Any idea who Ah Lon might be?"

Uday froze. "Ah who?"

"Ah Lon. He's mentioned in the messages."

Sayana interrupted, "No idea. We tried to guess but we knew you'd figure it out."

A soft voice replied, "Aaron. His name is Aaron. My son's nurse."

Sayana laughed. "Alleged nurse. You really got dad fooled, Tamara. Not us. We knew."

ASP Lee asked, "Knew what?"

"Aaron is her lover. Maybe her son's nurse, too, but her lover first. I'm sure you'll soon find out all the details, ASP Lee."

ASP Lee walked towards Tamara. "We'll need to take you in for questioning. I urge you not to resist as Sergeant Ridzwan handcuffs you." Tamara let out a piercing wail which had Wati and Conchita come crashing through the kitchen swing door, wondering what was happening. Uday noticed a hint of a smile on Wati's face as Tamara was led away, howling like a banshee, proclaiming her innocence.

Inspector Lim, who until then had observed the proceedings from a distance, approached Uday and his family. "We will need to ask you also to come in for questioning. Please make yourselves available. We'll be looking for Ms Tamara's daughter and the person known as Ah Lon in the messages."

27

Dr Low is standing with a nurse at the foot of Lavinia's bed when Uday enters the room, accompanied by Sayana, Ashwin and their wives. Angela looks pale, having had many sleepless nights since the police arrested Tamara. Apparently, Ashwin tried to convince her he really had no idea where Sharon was, but she didn't seem to believe him.

Five grief-stricken faces are looking at Lavinia. Priyanka and Angela are weeping.

"Mr Aurora, the signs show that Miss Lavinia is slipping away. We do not have much time for harvesting her organs—"

"Harvesting. Sounds like a business transaction. You can't think of a better word?" Sayana snaps, as Priyanka puts her arms around him.

Dr Low leans back and opens his mouth, as if searching for the right words. He pauses before speaking. "I'm sorry. I know this is very difficult and we are grateful that you agreed to donate Miss Lavinia's organs. We need to remove them while they are still functioning—"

Uday nods, "Give us some time with her, please. How long do we have?"

"I can only stretch it to thirty minutes."

"What about the priest?"

"He left just before you arrived. We called him right after we spoke to you. He happened to be in the next ward."

Sayana takes the first turn. As everyone leaves the room, Sayana calls out to Ashwin. "Shall we do this together?" There's an audible gasp. Angela pats Ashwin's arm as she releases her clasp of their intertwined fingers.

As Uday leads the women out of Lavinia's room, Ashwin and Sayana hug. I don't remember seeing them ever coming this close to being so affectionate to each other since they grew up. Sayana sobs into his brother's shoulders. Ashwin stares, glassy-eyed, at the wall in front of him. There are no tears, but I see immense sorrow, lined with guilt, in Ashwin's eyes. Ashwin pulls away and looks at Sayana, then sobs as he whispers, "Everything has changed, but it's going to be better now between us. I promise."

Sayana nods. "I hope so."

They both stand across from each other, at the top of Lavinia's bed. They take turns remembering moments from their childhood. Ashwin says, "Remember when you asked Mama to buy you a Singapore Airlines stewardess uniform to wear to a costume party? You were five or six. After that, you insisted on wearing it every time we flew on Singapore Airlines. We were all so embarrassed. I refused to walk near you, and even slapped your hand away when you tried to hold mine. After a few trips, Mama and Dad threatened to send you as an unaccompanied minor, but you outgrew the uniform before our next trip. What I would give to go back to that time and hold your hand as we walked through all those airports!" Ashwin reaches into his pocket for a handkerchief as he releases a soft sob. "Thank you for being the best sister anyone could ask for. Good night, my darling Lavi." Ashwin kisses her on her forehead and sinks into the armchair, sobbing.

Sayana continues staring at Lavinia for a few minutes after Ashwin stops speaking. every now and then moving his lips for a few seconds. It looks as if he has so much to say, yet nothing comes out. Sayana, the Cambridge-educated English teacher is now at a loss for words. I feel sorry for my younger son, yet I know this moment of humility is long overdue. "I am so sorry, Lavi, for not being a better big brother. I always loved you, adored you, and I know I could've done more for you … but I didn't. I am … I really am … thankful …" Sayana looks away and sobs, cupping his face in his hands. Shaking his head, he cries, "I am thankful you had Ashwin being the brother he was, making up for my failings, being there when I wasn't or couldn't be."

Ashwin walks to his brother's side and puts his arms around him. "Our ten minutes are nearly up. Say your goodbyes, Sayana."

Sayana kisses his sister's forehead. Again, he apologises and is led out by Ashwin, who holds the door open for Angela. Like her husband had done earlier with Ashwin, Priyanka asks to go in with Angela, wanting them both to have ten minutes together with Lavinia. But Angela refuses, preferring to be alone with Lavinia.

Angela sits on the armchair and closes her eyes, as if in prayer. She murmurs a few words in Chinese —a prayer, perhaps—before standing up and walking to the end of the bed. She tilts her head as she speaks to Lavinia. "My beloved Lavi, you are the most wonderful human being I have ever known. If ever I have been, or will be, as kind, or as thoughtful, as you, it will be because of you. Thank you for welcoming me as your sister. I shall never forget the day …" Angela takes a deep breath and begins to weep.

"That day … before Ashwin and I were to be married. You were nineteen, I was twenty-three. You gave me a plastic tiara from your old Barbie doll collection and told me that for years, you had been number one in Ashwin's life. You then hugged me and said I was now Ashwin's princess, and that you would settle for second position. I have never known such a generous spirit in anyone. Thank you, Lavi. Rest in peace."

I was there when Lavinia extended that warm welcome to Angela. I knew then that Angela would treat Lavinia like her own little sister. It was Angela's way of ensuring that Ashwin and Lavinia remained close.

Priyanka speaks the least amongst the four of them. She apologises for not making a bigger effort to be friendlier, she says she resented Lavinia for being the family star. Priyanka pats Lavinia's hand. "I realise now—a little too late—that you were just a lovely young woman making sense of this wicked world. Forgive me, Lavi." Priyanka does not cry but she bites her lip and shakes her head slowly as she runs her finger through Lavinia's hair. "Rest in peace, Lavi."

Uday knocks on the door before he walks in. Priyanka has another minute, but appears to be ready to leave. Uday pulls a chair from a corner of the room and places it as close as possible to Lavinia. He leans back and gazes at her with all the love a man can feel for his daughter.

"My clever, beautiful, child. I wish I could have protected you better, prevented this. I wish … I wish I had listened to you when you tried to warn me about … well, you know who. I shall not tell you what happened to the people who did this to you because you would be angry with me. You were always about forgiveness and justice. Some day I shall be more like you. For now, forgive me as I take pleasure in believing that the people who did this to you will rot in hell, while you will rest in peace."

Uday looks exhausted. The fire that was in him when he dropped by the other day, when he told Lavinia of his plans to send Tamara to jail, has been snuffed out. He now looks cold and hard. "You might have forgotten this, Lavi, but I haven't, along with your wish to donate your organs if you were ever in such a situation. Remember when your history teacher—Mr Menon, I think—passed away, and had left instructions for his body to be donated for medical research? You were fifteen, maybe sixteen. You had said it was such a thoughtful thing to do, the body being of no use to anyone once it's cremated. You had gone on to say that you would tell your children to plan the same for you." Uday sobs. It takes a few minutes before he stops heaving and tries to speak. He stammers, "I will do as you wish, my beloved Lavinia."

I place my hand on his arm. He does not respond. I go behind him and squeeze him as I wrap my arms around his shoulders. He looks towards the ceiling and closes his eyes. I run my fingers through his hair. He does the same, as if reaching for my hand.

It's nearly time, my love. Don't worry. She'll sleep peacefully in my arms.

"Oh, Julie … where are you? I miss you." Uday opens his eyes and looks at his watch. He stands and leans over Lavinia. "You have brought me nothing but absolute joy, but you must leave now. Tell your mother that no one else will ever take her place. Go to her now, Lavinia, light of my life. I will always love you. Rest in peace."

I release him from my embrace and lie down on my side next to Lavinia, my arm across her chest. Uday shivers as he stands, rubbing his arms to keep himself warm as he leaves the room, turning around to blow Lavinia a kiss as he shuts the door.

28

A Few Days Later

Uday arrived at the police station a little late. ASP Lee was waiting in his room, his hands in his pockets. His handshake was firm, and he made fleeting eye contact with Uday as he pursed his lips. The churn in Uday's stomach returned, the way it had when ASP Lee called him that morning, to be at the police station as soon as possible.

"Once again, Mr Aurora, I am very sorry for your loss."

"Thank you, ASP Lee. It's been very difficult for our family." Uday turned towards the window. The lush greenery from tall trees, and two pigeons on a ledge facing him briefly before turning around and flying away, did little to soothe his tumultuous mind.

"Nothing in the press so far. Let's hope to keep it that way. When this case goes to court, though, there'll be nothing we can do to stop reporters from covering it."

ASP Lee shrugged. "Right now, there isn't much to report anyway—very few facts and much speculation." He gathered his notes and placed them to one side. "As mentioned when we spoke, Miss Lavinia's death meant that the charges against Wang Yan—Tamara Wang's official name—were amended to instigation to commit murder."

"If found guilty, will she get the death penalty?"

"Most likely. The only problem now is the evidence. We have studied all the messages carefully. While it is possible to translate some code words to correspond to what we believe were part of Wang Yan's murderous plans, we cannot make assumptions or jump to conclusions without solid evidence."

"I understand. But you do have time to get more evidence, don't you?"

"We're working on it."

"Before we continue, tell me something, please. According to my son's army buddy, whose brother works at the prison, she shares a cell with another prisoner, and sleeps on a thin, unpadded straw mat which she has to unroll onto a cold concrete floor. No pillows, just two thin blankets, one of which may be rolled up and used as a pillow. Her cellmate rolls her out of her mat at 5am because she simply can't wake up. There's almost no privacy for the loo. The food is not great, and she's already lost some weight. She initially complained about her haircut being too ugly and the soap being too harsh for her skin, until she was slapped into shutting up. Is this true?"

ASP Lee smirked. "She does seem to feel entitled to special care. I don't think she's having an easy time at Changi Women's Prison. Especially being from China and bragging about her privileged past in the first ten minutes of being shown to her cell. A vast number of our prisoners are Singaporeans from humble backgrounds. Divas tend to be put in their place quite quickly."

Uday chuckled and considered his next question. Perhaps it was best not to ask. But he quickly changed his mind, thinking it might deflect any suspicion the police might have about him knowing her daughter's whereabouts. "What about her daughter? Any news?"

ASP Lee shook his head. "We're still looking. We know she was asked to cook at a private event, but we have no record of the caller or the address. The call was made from an Indonesian phone, so it was most likely a rich Indonesian tycoon entertaining some business associates. She was known to accept bookings outside of her off day, Monday, by taking leave or getting a medical certificate. This was one of those bookings. Apparently, her regular clients paid as much as a thousand dollars per evening for her to cook at their homes, usually for special guests."

Uday whistled, "Wow! It's true what they say about the Chinese—they can be quite lavish when it comes to food."

ASP Lee laughed. "Some of us, yes. I can't afford that kind of money. Besides, I like my street food and home cooked meals."

Uday nodded in agreement, though other than laksa, chicken rice and satay, he did not care much for Singapore's much lauded street food. With Sharon's body parts suitably disposed of without any chance of discovery, Uday was convinced he would never be a suspect in her disappearance. "What about the others? Lavinia was … assaulted … sexually …"

"The men, yes. We have detained the four people who took part in the attack. Three young men and a sixteen-year-old girl—"

Uday's eyes widened. "Sixteen?"

"Runaway, living with Sharon. Her parents never reported her missing. Probably a difficult teen whose parents were relieved when she left—"

Uday frowned. "What kind of parents would even think like that?"

"It's sad but we've seen such cases." ASP Lee glanced at the computer screen to his right. "All four confessed to their participation and identified Sharon Lin Zhang Min as the woman who hired them to carry out the attack. Two of the men were her colleagues at the restaurant—a chef and a waiter—the third one was a polytechnic student and the sixteen-year-old, Lee Hua, was Sharon's friend and flat mate. All four were promised two thousand dollars each to attack Miss Lavinia. None of them were paid—"

"So, they blabbed in revenge?"

ASP Lee shrugged. "Maybe. They were all picked up and questioned separately. Their narration of the events was the same."

Uday leant towards ASP Lee's table. "Is it possible that one of them sent me Sharon's phone? A wish for revenge, without realising the possible consequences?" Uday surprised himself with his convincing expression of feigned curiosity.

"It's possible, but they all denied any knowledge of sending Sharon's phone to you. Maybe it wasn't them. Also, admitting to it could implicate them in Sharon's disappearance. We're trying to find that link."

"I never figured out how they got Lavinia into the car. She regularly calls Grab taxi, so I'm surprised she'd get into a car with other people."

"Miss Lavinia used the shared ride service, which is cheaper. The attackers' car was waiting for her at the foot of the block, so it was there before her Grab ride arrived. She must have hopped in, assuming it was her ride, not bothering to check the car type or number plate, both of which were shown on her screen. The attackers had a phone with a Google map fixed to the windscreen, and the driver verified her name and destination. Just like in any private hire car."

"But how did they know where she was, and her timing?"

"Ah Lon, also known as Aaron—"

"What? No! He was part of this?"

"According to Lee Hua, the sixteen-year-old, yes. The men didn't know anything about him. Aaron only communicated with Sharon, who then gave all the instructions. Evidently, he knew her plans and her whereabouts, going as far as following her to her friend's place that Sunday—"

"He was supposed to be away!"

"He was in Singapore all along. Rented a cheap room somewhere, indulged in some heavy drinking and debauchery, evidently. He returned to your flat late the night of Wang Yan's arrest and found out about it from the guards. Looks like he sneaked into your flat, packed his bags and got himself on the next flight to England. He has British citizenship and knows that it will be much harder to be extradited to Singapore for a capital charge which carries the death penalty."

Uday waved his finger ferociously. "I knew it! There was always something sinister about that creep. I was dead against him moving to Singapore with her but ... oh well, what does it matter now?" Uday paused, trying to process this new twist in his never-ending nightmare. "That woman was jealous of my Lavinia, but to kill her? Was there anything else, ASP Lee?"

"The same girl told us that Wang Yan was angry when she found out about a will you had drawn up, to be effective on your wedding day. She mentioned a pre-nuptial agreement which she had refused to sign, and so you created this will as an alternative. Is this true?"

Uday nodded. "I ... I don't get it. How did she even know about the will? She must have been snooping around, going through my documents in my study, checking my emails ..." Uday's heart was beating rapidly. Tamara was obviously nothing like the woman he had believed her to be. "Perhaps she was recording our family discussions ..."

ASP Lee shrugged. "So many ways to get information these days, Mr Aurora. Especially when someone you trust goes digging. We were told Wang Yan believed Lavinia was conspiring with her brothers to force you to re-consider marrying her. She believed Lavinia was going all out to make things difficult for her. Is that true?"

"No! No, absolutely not! Well, yes, in that Tamara believed all that about Lavinia and yes, Lavinia did not like her, but that was more out of loyalty to her late mother. I assure you, ASP Lee, it is not at all true that Lavinia planned anything. The pre-nup and the will—my children came up with those, yes, but it was a wise idea to protect their inheritance should anything happen to me."

"You did set aside something for Wang Yan. Twenty percent?"

"Twenty percent was still a lot. She would have been very comfortable. But I suppose if she expected more, and believed it to be her right, then the idea of any percentage below her magic number would propel her into the deranged state in which she ended up."

"The will leaves sixty percent of all your assets to your three children, twenty percent to charity and twenty percent to Wang Yan. It seems that Wang Yan had expected everything, or at least half, to be left to her. We know that Wang Yan complained to her daughter, Sharon Lin, about the will. Based on what we've been told, Sharon only agreed to commit the murder to please Wang Yan, believing it might make her mother love her a little more."

ASP Lee leant forward and clasped his hands. "This will be very difficult for you, Mr Aurora, but please bear with me. Lee Hua told us that Miss Lavinia was taken to a roast meat factory to be ..." ASP Lee breathed deeply and stared at his table before continuing, "Hacked to pieces and roasted in the furnace."

"No! How could anyone plan such a violent death for my daughter? For anyone's sake?" The memory of seeing Lavinia on that cold, steel table with the hot furnaces in the corner, re-ignited an anger that made Uday's outburst seem really genuine.

"I'm sorry, Mr Aurora."

"And so Sharon decided to brutally attack my beloved Lavinia, let her die a painful death, and make her disappear? Without me or anyone in the family ever knowing what happened to her? Waiting years in the hope of finding her alive? All for her mother to love her more?"

The room was quiet for several minutes. Uday had lost his most precious child and ASP Lee was trying his best to be as sympathetic as possible.

"If things had gone according to Wang Yan's plan, then yes, this might have remained an unsolved crime. Wang Yan was so sure neither she nor her daughter would have been implicated in Miss Lavinia's disappearance. But … the situation changed and she's in jail while her daughter is missing."

"And my daughter is dead."

"I'm so sorry, Mr Aurora." ASP Lee stretched out his arms and clasped his hands across the table. "The roast meat man, known as Ah Huat … he's still on the run. Malaysian police will inform us once he's caught."

"But he didn't harm my daughter. He saved her."

ASP Lee grimaced. "We don't know the extent of his involvement. We'll still need him for questioning. The four people in remand said Ah Huat had betrayed them by not finishing the job. According to Lee Hua, Ah Huat was paid thousands of dollars." ASP Lee paused before walking to the door and asking his assistant to bring in two glasses of water.

"Looks like I'll be here for a while."

"Shouldn't take too long. Mr Aurora, I asked you to come in for another matter related to Wang Yan. Were you aware of the circumstances behind her husband's death?"

"Yes, of course. It was quite recent, less than a year ago. He was kidnapped, and even though she paid the full ransom, the kidnappers killed her husband. The three men involved were caught soon after and jailed, following an expedited trial. That seems to be all there is to it."

"There's a lot more to it, Mr Aurora. We contacted our counterparts in Shanghai, where Wang Yan was last known to reside. We were told that she is now a suspect in her husband's—"

"What? A suspect?" Uday rested his chin on his bent arm and stared at the tray of documents to his left. "After what she did to Lavinia, I suppose I shouldn't be surprised."

"They have gathered evidence and are now preparing extradition papers to charge her for instigating the kidnap and murder of her husband. Had they known Wang Yan was in Shanghai recently—"

"How could they not have known?"

"Wang Yan was travelling under an assumed name on a different passport. It was in her handbag, along with her official Chinese passport with her real name. Did you know she had one from the Dominican Republic? Under the name Chanel Li."

Uday flopped back into his seat and laughed mirthlessly. "No, I had no idea. What else do I not know about this woman?"

"I'm sorry, Mr Aurora. As I was saying, Wang Yan is wanted in China for her husband's murder. Of the three men arrested, one insisted he was innocent. Evidently, a prison warden believed him, and the police have now re-opened the case. It appears that Wang Yan and her friend, the nurse, Aaron Green, also known as

Ah Lon, hired three men to kill her husband. Two were arrested and charged, and are now waiting for their trial. The third man was her brother, who paid the allegedly innocent one to be the fall guy. Her brother remains free. I don't have the details but so far, there is evidence that Wang Yan planned the kidnap and murder, while her brother helped to execute the plan with Aaron—"

"I should have trusted my instincts and simply rejected her pleas to let him move to Singapore. Two murderers in my home! With him now in England, he'll get away with murder. Literally."

"Let's hope not. It may take years to bring him to justice, but let's hope you'll see the day."

Uday frowned, "Do you … do you think …" Uday shook his head forcefully. "No. No, I don't believe she would …"

"What is it, Mr Aurora?"

Uday took a few moments to gather his thoughts. "It's just as well I prepared the will. Even if she had not gone after Lavinia, she might have had the same plans for me. She might have staged a kidnap and had me killed, with the intention of being left a merry widow. She's clearly capable of it!"

"I don't know, Mr Aurora. It's possible, but we can't accuse her of what we think she's capable of. Right now, we'll continue our search for Sharon and Ah Huat, the man from the roast meat factory. Without their evidence, our investigations will be hampered."

"What if you don't find them?"

"We are quite sure we'll at least find Ah Huat. Even then, he is only tied to Sharon and not to Wang Yan. I'm sorry, Mr Aurora, but if we do not have sufficient evidence, we might not be able to procced with charging Wang Yan for instigating a murder."

"And she walks free? Just like that?" Uday thought of the

men who were released due to lack of evidence in the curry murder case.

"She will not walk free, Mr Aurora. If we do not have enough evidence to secure a conviction in Singapore, Wang Yan will be extradited to China where she will face charges for kidnap and murder. If found guilty, she could be executed, or sentenced to life imprisonment. There will be justice for Miss Lavinia."

"If you knew her like I do, life imprisonment would be worse than an execution. Far worse."

Uday felt cold and rolled down the sleeves of his linen shirt. He was grateful that circumstances had allowed him to torment Tamara with the belief that she had eaten parts of her daughter. He would have felt short-changed of the revenge he desired had she been arrested before she returned from China.

29

A Year Later

Uday answered a call from the hospital about the recipients of Lavinia's organs. The young man with cystic fibrosis who had received both Lavinia's lungs had died from an infection after five days. The other recipients had survived the full year and had high chances of surviving for the next five years, especially the two women who received Lavinia's kidneys. They were all very grateful and wanted to thank Lavinia's family for approving the organ donation.

The woman from the hospital's communications department, who introduced herself as Marina, spoke with a melodic lilt he had never heard in Singapore. Uday resisted the urge to ask where she was from, having heard his children complain over the years how annoying it was when people asked them the same question. It made them feel foreign and unwelcome, especially as the question was usually asked with more resentment than curiosity.

"Mr Aurora, would you like to attend an informal tea party in one of our meeting rooms? It won't last more than two hours, and our patients and their families are very keen to express their gratitude in person."

Uday could not think of a more arduous task than being

forced to make small talk and mingle with people who were alive because of his daughter's untimely death. There were five recipients, excluding the man who did not survive his lung transplant—a young man who received Lavinia's heart, a woman who received her liver, and the two women who received one kidney each. Lavinia's corneas helped a woman regain her sight. Along with their families, there would be too many people. There was only so much unsolicited gratitude he could handle, and he did not wish for anyone to feel beholden to him or to his family. Uday only did what Lavinia would have wanted.

"Thank you, Marina, but I don't think I could handle it. I'm very glad that my daughter was able to help so many people. That they are doing well is all the thanks my family needs." Uday asked her to convey his best regards to the patients and their families. He asked that she also explain to the patients that the circumstances would be too painful for him.

When Uday had heard the verdict about Tamara a few months ago—courts in China seemed to be particularly expedient in high-profile cases—he was relieved that she would not be executed. Having heard reports that organs from China's executed prisoners are used for transplants, Uday was sickened by the thought that her death would result in a continuing evil presence through several other lives.

"Nonsense, Dad, they're just organs," Sayana had said, and he was right, but it was a feeling Uday could not shake off.

He left the office and went home.

With a Scotch on the rocks in one hand, Uday flipped through the pages of a thick scrap book, filled from edge to edge with pictures from the time Lavinia was born until the day before the attack, when she had taken some pictures on her phone while out with friends. Selfies, or wefies, she had called them. Uday had asked Ashwin and Sayana to help him create a collection of photos and have them all printed so he could glue them into the scrapbook. Initially, he had looked at them every day. When the pain became too much to bear, he stopped looking at them altogether. Today, going through the scrapbook, reminiscing, Uday wept for his great loss.

When he reached the last page, Uday went through it again, stopping at each page, as if looking at the images for the first time. He stopped just before the middle, when he found a picture of Lavinia and her mother, taken when they were in front of the elephant enclosure at the zoo. Lavinia was six years old and was laughing while clinging to Julie's leg. He kept the page open, walked over to the bar to fix himself another drink, and plugged in his special collection of songs into the CD player.

Uday placed his feet on the coffee table, the one that Julie had bought, the one he retrieved from storage the day after Tamara was arrested. He sipped his Scotch as he tilted his head back, closed his eyes, and prepared himself for an hour of immersion in the compilation Ashwin and Sayana had created for him, starting with Lavinia's favourite song—Taylor Swift's *Romeo and Juliet*—and ending with one of Julie's favourites, an unlikely country number by a singer neither of them had heard of until her song became a hit. Julie liked it for the sentiment—the future she wanted for the children, where no matter how bad things were, they would overcome all their troubles with humility and grace.

Just before she passed away, Julie had asked Uday to write out the lyrics for each of their three children. She had specified the use of a fountain pen and paper from her writing desk—specifically from a box of heavy, textured, cream coloured paper from a well-known London stationer. Milled paper was a luxury Julie had allowed herself ever since her days of writing to her mother while she was at Edinburgh University. "Because Mum deserves it," she had said, when he first stood in line with her at the post office, waiting to stamp the envelope. It took Uday at least twenty attempts over several days to produce three perfect sheets—without smudges and spelling errors—of lyrics to the song, *I Hope You Dance.*

As he steeped himself in memories of Julie and Lavinia, while listening to an eclectic range of music in the stillness of his airconditioned living room, Uday felt a gentle breeze swish past. He touched his chest as a celestial shroud descended upon him. Uday smiled as he wiped away a tear, knowing he would never be alone.

Acknowledgements

Several people helped bring this book to fruition and I am grateful to every one of them.

Many thanks to my publisher and the team at Marshall Cavendish for their encouragement and collaboration throughout the process, from manuscript submission to completion. I am especially grateful to my editor, She-reen Wong, for her patience.

To Tara Dhar Hasnain, editor and friend, I am extremely grateful for your dedication and professionalism. Along with your sharp eye and magic touch, you made a significant difference to the manuscript.

To one of my editors, Daren King, thank you for your help with structure in the early incarnations of my manuscript. Your suggestions helped to take a rough draft and turn it into a novel.

To my friends, Sheila Wyatt and Nicola Yeo, thank you for being part of this development since the beginning, when I had barely finished Chapter 1. I was unsure about the idea but was determined to pursue it after our conversation.

Most of all, to my family – my husband and twin daughters. Thank you for reading my last draft and for always giving me the space and time to write.

About the Author

After nearly thirty years of working in advertising and the hospitality industry in Singapore, Mahita wrote her first book, *Praying To The Goddess Of Mercy: A Memoir of Mood Swings*, published in 2012. She now spends her time on mental health advocacy and pursuing personal interests including reading and writing. Her first novel, *Rain Tree*, was published in 2016. She is married and has twin daughters in their mid-twenties.

It Happened On Scrabble Sunday is her second novel.